AF446121

WHEN THE SHADOW MOVES

A Novel by Elise Caine

Sequel to WHEN THE SHADOW TAKES FORM

Dedicated to Pam and Denise,
For loving the first one so much.

Contents

A new day. A new job. A new life. Today was the start of it all for Jude Anderson. As she drove across the bridge spanning the Des Moines River and continued down Locust Street, her sense of excitement grew as she neared the building where she would work. Neat buff-colored stone blocks and huge darkly tinted windows overlooked the tidy sidewalk planted with trees every ten feet. It gave an impression of affluence and professionalism at the same time, not an easy combination to pull off she knew. It took careful consideration and planning to give that appearance. And a lot of continued maintenance. BICO had certainly achieved that look, and she hoped with all her heart that it was more than just skin deep. The two neatly framed diplomas in the small box she carried into the building, one a bachelor's degree in Mathematics and the other a master's degree in Statistics, gave Jude a sense of pride that she hoped would be enhanced by the company she would work for. The daughter of a Social Worker and a Teacher, ethics and social justice were as much a part of her DNA as the color of her dark brown hair which she currently wore in a neat bun on the back of her head. First day, first impressions, she had thought that morning as she had taken the time to pin the unruly curls up into the tight bun. Her outfit she had selected over the weekend, not a dull gray suit but a dark pair of navy pants and a pristine crisp white blouse with a stand-up collar. Not too flouncy and feminine because she didn't want that to be the first impression she gave. Men usually underestimated women they thought of as 'girly' and while she wasn't above using that to her advantage, the first day on the job was not the time to test it. Her 'uniform' as she thought of it would fit right in, the only indication of personal style was the soft brown Jimmy Choo shoes she'd chosen to wear. One of her few indulgences. Well, that and chocolate of course, but what woman didn't treat herself to some chocolate now and then? *Or every day?* And coffee, there was coffee too. There was always coffee.

Greeted pleasantly at the front desk by a tiny older woman who had chosen to wear her own hair steaked with gray loose in a short bob, Jude had been directed to one of the elevators in the lobby and told to go to the sixth floor. "Turn right after exiting the elevator and your office will be down that corridor" she'd been instructed. "Oh, and my name is Katherine, but everyone calls me Kate. You let me know if there is anything I can help you with. We'll get better acquainted in the future, I'm sure." Not wanting to seem unfriendly, Jude also hadn't wanted to immediately form a personal connection to the woman, who could very well be the root of the building grapevine, she knew. It was the ideal position, the perfect location for that sort of thing. So, she'd smiled kindly and simply replied "Thank you. If I need anything, I will let you know" as she pushed the button to close the elevator door. *Hhmmm* Kate had thought *not overly friendly, quiet, well mannered. That's the kind of girl who could do well at BICO. She will be interesting to watch.* The kind of girl she herself had been all those years ago when she'd started working for the company. *Over forty years ago, could it really be that long ago?* Few people ever guessed that the gentle elderly lady manning the reception desk of the main lobby owned a considerable share of stock in the company and held opinions that were respected and often sought by the upper management. An employee since day one, she knew more about the company than probably anyone else still working there. She knew the history of the company *and* of the people who worked there. She'd seen the current Vice President of the company grow from a small boy who came to visit his father into a man that she knew his father would have been proud of. She could have had one of those big fancy corner offices herself if she'd wanted it but had chosen instead to be stationed in the middle of everything, in a place where she could see all the employees come and go every day, where she could greet clientele and hear all the business happenings on a steady basis. Always careful not to repeat anything she heard, she did appreciate hearing the gossip that circulated in a business of that size, well, in a business of *any* size really. She had an almost sixth sense about people, often able to make an accurate opinion based on first impressions. It was a rare thing for her to reserve making that opinion after a single meeting, but she found herself doing just that when it came to Jude Anderson. Oh, she'd known the girl's name before it had been given, had already done her own research and found a photo on the web. Just the fact that Jude had been a little reserved without any indication of looking down on what she would have to think was a secretary had been in her favor. Kate had thought *She might do well. Only time will tell, but she might do very well here indeed. She didn't seem like one of the girls who came to work here purely as a means to find a wealthy husband. Or, worse yet, to find someone else's wealthy husband.*

Having excelled at the University in her chosen fields, Jude seemed to have almost a psychic ability to quickly assess and calculate risks and predict outcomes. Which is why she thought her new job as an actuary for a major insurance company was tailor-made for her. She didn't find the work boring and could often lose herself for hours when working on a project. Truthfully, Jude found much more success and satisfaction in her professional life than in her personal life. A little reserved in social groups, especially around strangers, she'd never been the sort of girl to attract much attention. *Any* attention really, not even from the boys in High School. As tall as most of them, taller than some, she was stick thin and hadn't worked hard with hair and makeup, wore the plain black framed glasses she preferred. Looks just had not been her priority. No, she had her sights set firmly on college and a bright academic and professional future. She knew she could find all the fulfillment she needed as long as she stayed on track. At the University, when the Freshmen "fifteen' had added a few curves to her shape, she had been oblivious to the looks that had started coming her way by the male students. She'd been so shocked the first few times she'd been asked out on a date or to go to a party that she'd just mumbled her way through excuses. More at home in the library than in the Student Union or stadium, she'd managed to get degrees in hand with little knowledge of the social aspects of upper education. And now here she was, in her very own office, albeit a small one, hanging those two black-framed diplomas on the wall. She made a mental note to pick up a plant and some generic but beautiful scenic art to add some color to the room. Maybe a modern pillow to place in one of the two gray tweed chairs that faced her desk. She wouldn't overdo, just add a little color and a little 'welcoming' feeling to her office. She knew she'd spend most of her time there alone, which was really fine with her, but she wanted to appear approachable and willing to take on any project where her particular skills would shine. Nothing too feminine, the decor needed to stay professional. She'd secretly thrilled to setting out her new office supplies, though, the one thing she bought too much of yet could never seem to get enough of. Colorful post-it notes and notebooks with motivational sayings on the covers, a new pair of rose 'gold' scissors and matching stapler, all set out on the desk beside her computer. A mousepad and wrist cushion with a matching white and gray marble design, with just a few streaks of metallic rose gold to match the other accessories. She knew it was silly, but just seeing the brand new fine-point ink pens in the cup on the edge of her desk gave her pleasure. *You're pathetic* she'd thought to herself chuckling. And then got down to business. Lost in the numbers, she'd jumped slightly when there'd been a light tap on the door and a pretty blonde woman had stepped into her office.

"Hi. Welcome to BICO. My name is Carrie and I have the office right across the hall from yours. Your door has been closed all day, so I hadn't been able to catch your attention." "Oh, I'm sorry" Jude had started to apologize although she wasn't sure exactly what she was apologizing about. "No, no, I didn't mean it to come out that way. I'm always a little nervous meeting new people, something I promised myself I would work on. So, I thought I'd come over and introduce myself. But of course, I made a wrong step right off the bat." Jude smiled more sincerely this time, surprised that the woman who looked like she had been a high school cheerleader could be deprecating and sincere about her own faults. Although it wasn't really a fault in Jude's mind, she herself was always careful around strangers. "Look, let's start all over," Carrie had continued, hardly taking a breath. "My name is Carrie Sanders and I have the office right across the hall from yours. I'm a Junior Underwriter, and I know you're the new Actuary. Welcome to BICO. I noticed that you hadn't taken a break today and thought maybe you would like to get some lunch with me?" Jude's first instinct was to decline, she knew it was always a bad idea to form work friends too quickly, but with Carrie standing there nervously chewing on her bottom lip, Jude just didn't have the heart to say 'No.' Added to that, her stomach let out a loud growl right at that moment, having just woken up at hearing the talk about food apparently. It was almost one o'clock and she really hadn't taken a break or eaten anything all morning. Laughing at the sound, she'd quickly decided "Sure, I'd like that. I don't really know the area yet and haven't had time to look for restaurants near work." "Well, there's the cafeteria on the first floor but unless you are really pressed for time, I wouldn't recommend it very highly. Your common fast-food restaurants all within a block or two of here, but I'm trying to keep away from the extra calories and fat. There's a nice deli right around the corner actually, that usually isn't too busy, especially since we are going in a little later and may miss most of the lunch crowd. It's called Captain's, although I'm not exactly sure why. Good sandwiches on crusty breads with lots of spread choices, they also have a little salad bar that I usually go for."

He'd noticed the two women getting onto the elevator one floor down from his. Of course, he'd seen the dumb one before, that was how he thought of the little blonde. Probably not a brain in her head. Stupid whore. The other one he'd never seen before. Taller with dark hair and black glasses, she looked a bit like a librarian. In a company this big, he'd seen so many come and go. Especially the women. It was like a revolving door. Who knew if this new one would last? He hadn't made eye contact and neither woman had made an effort to engage with him. The dumb one had just continued right on talking. "So, you said you weren't familiar with the area. Does that mean you've moved here from someplace else?" "Yes, well, I'm in the process of moving, actually. From Ohio. Columbus, Ohio. I took an apartment just for two months to give myself time to see if the job was, well, I mean, if I was a good fit for the job. And to get to know the area better to find out which parts of town were the best for safety, shops, restaurants, and proximity to work of course. Most of my stuff is still in storage in Ohio. I figured I'd make a trip back within the next month and pick everything up. Fly there, bring everything back in a U-Haul. I don't really have that much to bring. I'm a little intimidated to drive one of those moving vans, but I think I can manage with one of the smaller ones..." she'd continued talking as they stepped off the elevator ahead of him.

He'd watched them walk away. Every step. He'd thought about the dumb one before. About making her a target. She'd be easy enough to do. Too easy. It had been too long. There'd been that one outside of Stroudsburg, Pennsylvania he'd done on his drive across country from Providence to Des Moines. He'd noticed her getting into her car at a truck stop along the highway, still wearing an apron from her morning shift. He'd followed her to a rundown motel, the kind that rented rooms by the month, had easily gained access since there was no security. It has been so easy. Had barely slowed his trip west at all. And then there was the one he'd done in Starved Rock State Park in Illinois. She was young. Had made the mistake of chatting with him when he'd gone into the Lodge and Conference Center to pick up brochures, thinking it might be a nice place to bring his nephews on a future vacation. She was staying with friends in the Starved Rock Cabins not far from the Visitor Center, she told him. He'd politely asked if she liked it there, if the cabins were kept clean, indicating that he was thinking about bringing his nephews there, and did she think they would like to stay in the cabins? The entire conversation spontaneous for him, as the thoughts ran through his mind. No sense in lying, he'd thought, when the truth was useful. She'd gone on to say that her friends were out on the trails that day, but that she had stayed behind because she'd sprained her ankle the day before. He'd thanked her and mentioned that he might drive over and have a look at the cabins. That way, he was covered if she noticed him there later. He hadn't had the luxury of watching those two, learning their routines. He hadn't known their names before the kills. They just weren't that important. He was experimenting. Something had gone wrong in Providence, there had been something to tip the cops off. And he'd been so careful, always choosing diverse targets with no ties to each other or to him. But there had been something. He had to be more careful. Smarter. Change what he needed to change.

And then there was the one he'd done after he'd settled in here. He'd given himself a solid six months to commit the city layout, the streets and buildings to memory. In new territory, he might make a mistake. And that would never do. So, he'd taken the time to become familiar with the city, to settle in. He'd found a house to rent, an average white ranch-style house in an old neighborhood, not too trendy. Just an average-looking house. But it had one exceptional quality that excited him. The full basement, something he hadn't had in Providence. The owner had explained that most houses in the Midwest had them, as a safe place to go during a tornado. So, down a long flight of thirteen steps, he now had a dark basement with no windows, housing the furnace and little else in the room at the bottom of the stairs. But there was a second, smaller room to the back. Even darker, even emptier. Lit only by a bulb hanging from the ceiling with no cover, the light switch outside the door. *Interesting,* he'd thought. *This might work out really really well,* as he'd told the man he would take the rental. Just what he wanted. He'd given himself time to get comfortable in his new job, time to allow the other workers to stop thinking of him as the new guy. People remembered a new guy. He'd seen her getting into a car downtown, outside a trendy coffee shop, carrying one of those dome-shaped cups in her hand. He'd followed her with his car until she'd pulled into a driveway, into the garage. He drove on by, committing the address to memory, the look of the house, the layout of the shrubbery in the yard. Overgrown leafy bushes lined the front of the house, a perfect hiding place. He wouldn't drive by again, wouldn't take a chance on someone seeing a strange car in the neighborhood more than once. One time was easy enough to shrug off, someone lost. Two times in the same car, not as easy to explain away. No, he did his surveillance on foot, parking his car in a strip-mall parking lot about five blocks away from the house. He'd borrowed his nephews' dog Charlie and walked him along the way, just an ordinary guy walking his ordinary dog. A pet lover. All guys who liked pets were good, right? Safe? People saw what they wanted to see. Of course, he hadn't taken Charlie when he did the actual job, Charlie was just for cover so he could scope out her routine and location. Her name had been Sarah. It had been entirely too easy to gain access through a set of sliding doors on the front deck late one night. Entirely too easy to slip unheard into her bedroom. Thank goodness she hadn't had a dog; the thought had almost made him laugh out loud. He was that giddy with excitement. But still he was careful, he'd told himself he was still smart enough to get away with it. No evidence, no connection to him. He'd slipped back out just as quietly, maybe a bit quicker, and had disappeared into the night. That had been almost a year ago. And he could feel an edginess coming over him, something that hadn't happened in the past. Still, he could control it, he knew that. It wasn't like he got pleasure from killing, not at all. It was just something that had to be done, something he had to do since no one else was doing it. The whores had to die, all of them, that's all. It was very clear to him.

Kate noticed the two women come off the elevator together, chatting. *Well, isn't that nice?* she thought, *Carrie has already met the new girl and invited her to lunch.* That was progress, she knew, for Carrie. Not so long ago she wouldn't have even introduced herself to someone new, let alone made plans to share lunch. Some people thought she was outgoing, but Kate knew most of that was just nervousness. It also gave some people the impression that she was 'dingy,' but Kate also knew that wasn't the case. It had taken her awhile to get Carrie to open up, even a little, even enough to greet her each morning on the way past her reception desk. But she knew Carrie to be kind, probably one of the kindest people she'd ever met because Carrie didn't broadcast it. It had been three years ago when Carrie had overheard one of the Senior VPs wishing Kate a 'Happy Birthday' at the desk as she had been walking past on the way to the elevator. That afternoon, when she had returned from lunch, Kate had been surprised to find a pretty cupcake with pink icing and sprinkles on her desk waiting for her. No card or note, she had no idea who had left it for her. It had taken her a few days to guess that it might have been Carrie, she remembered that she was near when Jason had mentioned her birthday that morning. But if Carrie wanted it to be a secret, a surprise, Kate could go along with that. It was a really nice gesture.

Kate had been surprised when her birthday had rolled around the next year to come in to find a cupcake already on her desk, this one was chocolate with chocolate icing and tiny white star candies on top. Amazed, Kate couldn't believe that Carrie would remember the date a whole year later. She must have made note of it in her planner. And wasn't that just the sweetest thing, to pay attention to someone she really didn't know, to try to make that someone have a lovely day on her birthday? And again, the third year she'd found yet another cupcake on her desk. Yes, she'd decided that Carrie really was one of the few genuinely nice people on the earth. She'd worked some, without pushing, to get the girl to open up a little. And Carrie did seem to have gained some confidence over the past few years. She had relaxed a little, maybe because she was becoming more comfortable at her job. Kate worried a little that the new hire, Jude was her name, would make assumptions that would eventually hurt Carrie. But then, maybe Kate herself was making assumptions about Jude. She'd just have to wait – and watch – and see how things would progress there. At first glance, Jude also seemed a little shy, she was quiet and reserved, not the type to intimidate Carrie. So, it might be a good friendship. Both girls probably needed that. She knew that Jude was new to the area and probably didn't know anyone there. And Kate felt that Carrie could use a little kindness in return for her own. She hoped it would work out.

Jude felt she had settled well into the new job after a month, settled enough to know she liked the work and the company. She'd been impressed that she hadn't seen any indication of questionable ethics. So many big businesses could 'talk the talk' but when it came down to it, most were willing to break rules when the end result was higher profits. But she hadn't gotten that sense at BICO. And she found that she liked the people too, although she didn't interact with many considering her job. Which in some ways was a plus to her thinking. Carrie had become her regular lunch date. They were comfortable talking about work and things in general, though neither had offered much personal information. And she had developed the habit of stopping at the main desk each morning for a few words with Kate. She'd been pleased to find that Kate never shared any company gossip with her, which meant Kate wasn't sharing any gossip *about* her. And of course, she knew there was always gossip when a new person started. Kate didn't ask personal questions either, even after a month of working there. And maybe that was why she found herself actually occasionally *offering* bits and pieces of personal information to Kate. When she'd talked to her about finding the best area of town for a more permanent apartment, Kate had advised the parts of town she definitely needed to stay away from. In the end she had suggested one of the newer trendy townhouses that were within a few blocks of the company or, for a totally different option, one of the condos that had been put into the old brick warehouses down by the river. She'd been pleased when Jude had been the most interested in the warehouse condos and ultimately that is where she had settled. Signing the purchase contract had given her a twinge of uncertainty but she'd taken the plunge anyway.

She'd loved the huge floor-to-ceiling windows that filled the entire condo with light. And the night view of the city lights was like a picture. She could just see the modern pedestrian bridge that arched over the river. While she found the view she had of the river calming, the opposite direction afforded views of the trendy new pedestrian-only street with the quirky shopping and restaurant options which always provided entertainment. She liked watching the people come and go, liked hearing the music drift up from the street musicians, and appreciated the trees and plantings that had been installed to make the old industrial area seem fresh. She'd managed to get one of the condos on the top floor, how she lucked into that she'd never understand, it must just have been good timing. So she had roof access and was considering creating a little oasis with planter boxes and a small bistro table and chairs up there. She'd have to get advice though, not knowing what to plant to withstand the winds or winter weather, considered that it might just have to be annual plantings. Winters in Iowa were probably just as harsh as they had been in Ohio. Which was fine, bright bursts of color in equally colorful pots would do. But the thought was there to possibly do a long planter with several columnar evergreens, to block off the view from the other condos. Or a trellis system with vines, that might work better. Just something to act as a screen so she could enjoy her green space without being on display. She'd definitely have to visit a home-and-garden center to get some ideas. And she'd have to talk to the building management to make sure what was allowed and what was not, but she wasn't thinking too differently from the patio areas she saw outside some of the other condos. She didn't want to hire a landscape company, this was something she wanted to do herself, *for* herself. It might be a pain to haul bags of potting soil from the condo up the stairs leading to the roof, and she knew that ongoing she would have to carry water on an almost daily basis. Hhmmm, she might watch a few U-Tube videos about drip irrigation, thinking she would probably be really glad at some point in time if she installed one. Better to do that at the beginning, she'd thought.

She'd also loved the exposed brick walls in the condo, feeling it just gave a warmth and sense of history and time to everyday life. Mostly an open space, only the two bedrooms and baths were walled in. The original wood floors had been refurbished at some point in the past, recently enough that they were in good shape but long enough ago that you could see some scratches and imperfections. Jude found she liked those imperfections. Decorating had been a bit of a challenge since there were not many walls to place furniture against, she'd never lived in what they called an open concept before. She'd bitten the bullet after a month at the new job and flown back to Ohio to pick up her belongings. The drive back in the U-Haul truck had been more than a little scary, but she'd survived and could add that to her list of life accomplishments, though one she did not think she would ever care to repeat. No, next time, if there was a next time, she would hire a moving company no matter the cost. She had a few old pieces that she had held onto from her grandmother, a long carved sideboard and what had been called a 'Library' table that Jude liked to use as a desk. And the new bed she had bought no more than a year before moving, the one she had fallen in love with in an antique store window with the black iron frame. Most of her other large pieces of furniture she had sold or given away rather than pay for storage. She'd tried to only keep the things she had a personal attachment to. Smart move, she'd decided after driving the *smaller* U-Haul truck for about an hour, she really didn't think she could have managed one of the bigger ones. She'd hauled up all the boxes herself after hiring local movers to bring the large furniture pieces up on the freight elevator with the ornate Art Nouveau grill. And had been so very thankful for that elevator to eliminate at least a few of the trips up and down. And up and down. And appreciated it again when the new furniture she'd purchased had started to arrive. The real puzzle had been exactly *where* to place the couch, the dining table and chairs. In the end she'd moved the couch three times, let it sit in one spot for another week before moving it a fourth time so that it was facing the windows. It looked a little odd out in the middle, not against a wall, but she knew she wanted the light and to see the view from the couch. An old rug from a thrift store placed in front of the couch had helped, as had the two mismatched French Country side chairs she had recovered in solid cream fabric. It had continued to feel odd until she'd spotted a gleaming table with intricate inlaid designs in one of the consignment shops down the street. Seen and fell in love with, on the spot. She'd only haggled half-heartedly with the shopkeeper, settling for just ten dollars off, she wanted it that badly. And the shopkeeper had even offered to deliver, at least to the bottom floor of her building. Once in her condo, she'd set the tall table behind the sofa, added the vintage Tiffany lamp that had belonged to her grandmother, a small stack of books to elevate a vase which held a bright, fresh bouquet she'd picked up in the grocery store. Although Tiffany, the lamp did not have great value because of a crack that ran most of the way down the base, but it was precious to Jude because it had belonged to her grandmother. So precious, in fact, that she'd driven with it in the front seat beside her on the trip from Ohio to Iowa. Satisfied, finally, that the couch looked like it belonged, she'd added some mixed-pattern pillows and a soft throw blanket. *Now* it felt right, it looked warm and cozy. Not necessarily the farmhouse decor trend that was so popular, but it felt like *her.* It was not like all that many people would see it anyway. She only had to make herself happy. Two stacks of books served as a table of sorts between the chairs since her homes had always been overflowing with books. The floor to ceiling built-in bookcases along the south wall of the condo had been another of the selling points for her. Now they were almost filled completely with her books, covering such a wide variety of her interests that she sometimes wondered what impression they would give a stranger. Not that she cared. She loved reading about archaeology and history, loved cookbooks too and just would not part with some of her favorite novels that she had read too many times to count over the years. There was fine classic literature and new dime store fiction. Her reading collection was as diverse as she was. A few family photos, a large piece of white coral she's bought on her first – and last – trip to Florida, and a pottery urn filled with succulents added to the bookcase, but she knew those would probably end up elsewhere as more books found their way into the condo, somehow that just always seemed to magically happen. A big cushy leather chair worn from time, a faded red Persian rug, a small table and one of those arching overhead lamps made for a cozy reading nook. None of the rugs in the open space matched, they were all different designs, from different parts of the world, but she thought they combined to make a colorful setting. Most were faded, a little worn, and she liked that feel. Turning in a circle, *it looks good,* she thought. *No, it looks right, and that's even better.* It felt new and fun, but it also felt like home, and how often did you get that all at the same time?

It had taken Carrie almost four months to work up the courage. But she'd decided to take the chance. "Good morning, Jude," she'd smiled nervously as she came through Jude's office door, which was seldom closed anymore. "I was just wondering, if you aren't busy, or don't have something else to do, if you might want to come over to my house on Saturday afternoon for dinner? No pressure, if you're busy I totally understand. If you want to." Jude saw the tell-tale sign of Carrie chewing on her bottom lip, had come to realize this habit was most noticeable when she was nervous. "Sure, Carrie. I'd really like that. Just give me directions and I'll try not to get lost on the way. What time and what should I bring?" The smile, a real smile, bloomed on Carrie's face "Oh, you don't have to bring a thing. And I'll email you directions from the internet. It's not too hard to find. Thank you for saying you'd come. My Sam has been saying we needed to have people over but, well, I guess you can imagine I wouldn't be comfortable in a crowd or having a party, even at my own place. Sam loves to cook on the grill, so it'll just be informal. Dogs and burgers if that's OK? Or I can stop off and pick up steaks or pork chops or chicken or really anything you would prefer." Jude held up her hand in a 'stop' motion

"Carrie, dogs and burgers sounds just perfect! I haven't had anything cooked on a grill in so long, now you're making my mouth water. This will be fun. Oh, and Carrie?" Carrie had already been out the door heading to her office to look up the driving directions when she turned back, "Yes, Jude?" "Thanks Carrie. I just wanted to say Thanks. This is really nice of you."

That Saturday, promptly at 4pm, Jude had knocked on the door of a cute little house painted a soft yellow with Aegean blue shutters. *It even looks like Carrie,* she'd thought. Seconds, literally seconds, later, Carrie had opened the door. "Hi. Come on in. Oh," she'd noticed the big bowl Jude was carrying "you made potato salad, how thoughtful, I didn't think of that." "Well," Jude said with a grin, "I made potato salad if by that you mean I *made* a trip into the store to pick some up, then yes, I guess you can say I made potato salad." Laughing now, more at ease, Carrie led the way through the living room into the small tidy kitchen. "Oh, I know it isn't fancy," she said, "but I just wanted someplace homey feeling and Sam and I are happy here. The neighbors are nice and it's quiet on this street. Oh, and speaking of Sam, how rude of me, let me get you something to drink and then we'll go on outside so you can meet Sam. What would you like? I have lemonade, iced tea – both sweet and unsweet – sodas, sparkling water, I just wasn't sure what you would want to drink so I got options." Walking out minutes later with a tall glass of iced lemonade that tasted like pure sunshine, Jude smiled at the man in the wheelchair beside the grill. "Jude, this is, well, this is Sam. And Sam, this is Jude from work." Shrugging at herself, "Oh my, I butchered that introduction, didn't I? Of course, this is Jude from work, you knew Jude from work was coming over." Knowing Carrie was starting to work herself up, Sam had simply reached across, taken her hand, and smiled at Jude. "Hi Jude from work. I'm Sam, it's really nice to meet you and welcome to our home. How do you like your burgers cooked?" Smiling, you couldn't help but smile at someone who so clearly adored Carrie, Jude had replied "Hi Sam. It's nice to meet you too. And thank you for having me over. I like my burgers to still have a little *moo* left in them if that's manageable. It's almost impossible to get beef cooked rare in restaurants anymore, they're afraid of lawsuits. I promise, girl scouts' honor, that I will not sue you if my burger has more pink than brown in the center." Sitting at the pretty round table Carrie had set with colorful napkins and flowers in a vase, they'd easily fallen into conversation, talking about how Jude was settling in, about how Sam didn't get the chance to try his cooking experiments on anyone except Carrie. Swallowing the first big bite of burger with gooey cheese on top, Jude had laughed "Call me. Anytime. Anytime you need someone to experiment on. I love to try new foods, love comfort foods, love home-cooked meals, really, I just love eating in general." Carrie had smiled at her friend,

"It's true, I know it's true, because I watch her eat the biggest lunches you've ever seen, *every* day, and she never seems to gain an ounce. Unlike me, where every calorie goes straight to my hips. I really do not know where you put it all." "Must just be my metabolism," Jude had answered, "but it wasn't always a blessing. When I was a teenager, I was taller than most of the boys in my class and too skinny. No one ever wanted to date me." "Oh, but you're not too skinny now," Carrie protested, "I'd say you are more 'willowy.' Yes, that's a good word. Actually, I'm not sure if it *is* a word or not, but it's what you are. Tall and willowy."

During the meal and afterwards, Jude realized that Sam was the perfect counterpart to Carrie. Calmer, definitely more secure, he was clearly someone that would support Carrie. Someone who would take care of Carrie, making sure nothing ever hurt her. That was the feeling she got and it made her instantly like Sam, but she found as the evening went on that she genuinely did like his personality too. They shared an interest in old black and white movies, in food, and in books. After dinner Sam had invited Jude into his office where Jude saw books and more books. "Wow. I didn't think I'd ever meet anyone with more books than I have. It's like an addiction, isn't it?" And, as she'd read through some of the titles "Oh, I have this one too. I just love the ending; it was so unexpected. Don't know why I keep it, because now I know the ending of course, but just can't part with it. I should donate it." "Look Jude," Sam had hesitantly started "since we're alone right now, I want to thank you. To thank you for being so kind to Carrie. For being her friend. For all the lunches and for coming over today." "Sam, you don't have to thank me for any of that. I really like Carrie. She was the first person here who offered to be my friend." "Maybe, but I'd bet it's easier for you to make friends than it is for Carrie. You're the first person from work she's ever had over. Other than my family, I think you may really be the first person ever. I'm not telling any secrets, but she didn't always have the easiest childhood and making friends is hard for her. It's hard for her to overcome her anxieties. I'm just glad she took a chance on you, that's all. And I think she worries about how people will react when they meet me, when they understand about us, that we're a couple. Not that she is embarrassed, but I know in her mind that she worries that I could be hurt by something someone might say. But the truth is, nothing can hurt me as far as Carrie is concerned, she's perfect. Perfect for me." And, seeing that simple truth in Sam's brown eyes, Jude had smiled back.

It had been on the drive home after dropping Jared and James off from a movie that he had seen her. Stopped at a red light, at first he actually didn't see her. Likely, if what looked like a dark pile of blankets laying back in a recessed store entry hadn't moved, he never would have even known there was a person there. He'd watched a filthy old woman crawl out from the blankets, greasy gray hair and layers of dirty clothes, she looked like the worst nightmare he could imagine. Way worse than the monster in the movie he had just taken his nephews to see in the giant mega theater complex. He had no sympathy for the homeless, especially a homeless woman. Clearly, she had failed in life, failed at all the things a woman should not fail at. If she'd been a good wife, a good mother, even a good daughter, she never would have ended up searching through dumpsters for food and clothing. He didn't buy all the bleeding-heart social workers who did TV interviews and tried to explain that the homeless problem in America was more about mental illness than about a lack of motivation. That people just didn't understand. He'd noted the location, the storefront which clearly was out of business. He knew the whore would probably move around, but also knew that if she'd found a place she thought was safe, was out of the wind and rain, she might stay there regularly. And he had seen her again the next night and the next as he'd driven the same route. He'd followed her slowly the following evening, driven around the block a few times because she walked so slowly, but he had seen her cross the street and go inside one of the food kitchens that offered meals for the homeless. He'd parked across the street and sat for the 38 minutes she was inside, watching her come out and head right back to her spot. He knew he'd never be able to find out her name, or really anything else about her, but he knew enough. Enough to know that she had to die, and a high-pitched giggle had escaped him when he'd thought it through and came to the conclusion that the police probably wouldn't even search very hard for her killer. It was one less problem for them. One less burden on society. He was doing them a favor.

He'd dressed the part. Even though it disgusted him, he'd dug a ratty old hoodie out of a bag of clothing left in one or those mobile clothes donation boxes. He'd not showered or brushed his teeth on Friday or Saturday or Sunday morning. He really couldn't risk going any longer than that because he didn't want to miss any days of work, something that might show on his employee record. Dug out his oldest pair of jeans, adding a few strategic rips and rubbing garbage from his trash can into the denim. He'd purchased a drab olive-green trench coat from one of the Salvation Army stores he'd passed during his drive across county, *just in case* he'd ever need it. Lord, he stunk. It was enough to make him literally gag. *Mom would have thrown a fit.* One benefit to the disguise was that with all the layers of clothing, it was easy enough for him to hide the baseball bat underneath the trench coat in a way that wasn't noticeable. Especially since he knew most people didn't pay attention to vagrants, which he hoped to appear to be, they were a source of embarrassment. Most people didn't want to see the homeless or the hungry if they were not willing to offer shelter or food themselves. Guilt. The homeless were invisible because of other people's guilt.

He'd approached her slowly, staying close to the buildings with a forced limp, leaning heavily on the support. He walked hunched over, like he was trying to shield some of the cold autumn wind. Forcing a hacking cough, he knew she'd heard him coming, was watching him approach from about a block away. She hadn't run away, although he could tell as he drew nearer that she was wary. *You should be afraid*, he'd thought. He'd let her watch him, made her think that he had just then seen her. He had stopped, acting afraid himself. He'd stumbled across the road to the other side, making her think she was safe. Maybe that he was a harmless drunk. He'd continued on down another two blocks, turned the corner and backtracked along the alley that ran behind the old buildings. Creeping along the side street closest to where he knew she was lying; his anticipation was growing. His pulse was beating so loudly in his ears he was amazed no one could hear. This time she didn't see him coming. She was asleep or unconscious, he'd thought. Mistakenly as it turned out, because she'd screamed and started to run away when he was no more than five feet from her. *Damn.* He'd lunged, grabbed the outermost layer of clothing with one hand, had swung the bat with the other. He'd known right away that she was dead, the bashing of the bat into her skull had pretty much eliminated any possibility of survival. He'd let her drop right there on the sidewalk, had walked away, still limping, until he'd turned the corner into the side street when he'd quickly increased his pace until he got to his car. Thankful for the darkness, he'd removed the clothes and placed them into the garbage bag before he'd climbed behind the wheel, trying to reduce chances of fiber evidence, although he knew it was unlikely that anyone would ever check his car since there was no way to connect him to the murder. As always, the clothing he burned along with the gloves. He was confident that his car hadn't been parked where any security camera might be, it really was a derelict part of town. Just to cover all bases, and that pun cover all *bases* had made him laugh out loud uncontrollably, he'd covered over the license plate with enough mud to make the numbers illegible. He'd always specified license plates with just numbers, none of those cute vanity plates, because he knew it was harder for any potential witnesses to remember a string of meaningless numbers. He'd found himself unable to sleep that night, which had just irritated him because he had to go to work the next morning. He'd taken a shower of course, the minute he got home, but thought he could still smell some of the odors. As he lay in bed, he relived the evening events, something nagging in his mind. Had he missed something, forgotten to do something? Unable to pinpoint exactly what it was, he'd tossed and turned for hours before drifting off just before the alarm clock had gone off.

Jude was finding more and more to like about her new city. It wasn't too big or overwhelming. There was a coziness to it, despite the size. And everyone was friendlier in the Midwest, she decided. She even liked her job. Left mostly to herself, she could lose herself for hours in the work. And she liked the friends she had already made. She'd had dinner at Sam and Carrie's house so often that she'd felt compelled to have them over to her place. To return the favor. She didn't have Sam's skill with a grill, well, she didn't have a grill at all. But maybe that was a thought for the rooftop sanctuary she was creating. If it was allowed. Nor did she have the patience to prepare Carrie's comfort food meals, though they were something she had come to look forward to. Sam had easily been able to get to the condo on the freight elevator, another plus she hadn't considered when taking it. She'd ended up making a simple pesto pasta with chicken, shaved parmesan cheese on top, served it with a salad and some rustic crusty bread she had picked up at the bakery down the street. Her best recipes were simple. Maybe she needed to take a cooking class. The more she thought about it, the more she warmed to that idea. She'd have to find out what was available in the city.

And so it was that two weeks later Jude found herself in the pristine professional kitchen of Sylvia, of 'Cooking with Sylvia.' Sylvia had apparently at one time hosted a local cooking show that played in the afternoons just before the 5 o'clock news. Everything was stainless, even the countertop that Jude found herself sitting at. It was sterile, should have felt sterile and cold, but Sylvia, or her setup crew, had placed rustic and high-end kitchen items around the area which gave it some personality. Two huge wooden cutting boards, one round and one a long rectangle, were propped against the backsplash. Pots of herbs were growing in the windowsill. Jude could recognize rosemary and parsley, thought she knew basil in another, but the others were unknown to her. She'd have to learn them. One of those shiny and expensive Kitchen Aid stand mixers in a dark red was sitting on a back counter. And Jude knew enough to recognize the flame-colored Le Creuset stockpot sitting on the stove. Her cousin Alice had asked for one on her wedding registry. Jude had been shocked at the price, even if it was from France. Knife blocks, food processors, all the tools of the trade were spread out pleasingly around the large kitchen. A double wide refrigerator and an extra-large dishwasher were along one wall, while three ovens were set into the other wall. The cooktop itself was imbedded in one of the biggest islands Jude had ever seen. A good setup, she thought, for a cooking show. Although she couldn't help feeling that she might be a little out of her league. The advertisement had called it an intermediate class. As she was wondering whether she should have joined a beginners' class, two other women came in the door and found places on some of the other barstools at the counter where Jude sat. Clearly, they already knew each other because their conversation hadn't stopped from the time they entered the door through the time they sat down and still it continued. It was then that Sylvia had come in from a side door, a plump middle-aged woman wearing a bright blue apron with colorful flowers embroidered on it. Greeting her students warmly, she chit-chatted a little to get them to open up about themselves, to make them more comfortable before the class. After a few minutes and glancing at the clock, she'd began "Well, I was expecting one more, but I see it is seven o'clock exactly and I'm not one to wait for latecomers. I strongly believe in punctuality, so..." Just then, the entrance door had opened one last time. Jude heard footsteps approach behind her and then turned just as their last student joined the group and took the stool next to hers. "Sorry I'm late," he said with an easy smile that quickly won Sylvia over, "I hope you didn't wait long. Traffic coming across town was worse than usual today. First snowfall and you'd think everyone had forgotten how to drive on it." It was easy to see why Sylvia was won over, as were the other two women in the class. Not classically handsome, he had thick sandy hair and eyes that were that impossibly bright shade of blue. Eyes that sparkled a little as he'd apologized to Sylvia, to the group, when a dimple appeared in his left cheek as he smiled. Just in his left cheek. No, not handsome. Not what you would call 'cute' either, since he was tall with wide shoulders and slim hips, too well built to be called 'cute.' But there was something about Jake that drew people, especially women, to him. He unwound the beige woven scarf from his neck and smiled at the two older friends at the end of the counter that seemed to stretch for a mile, at least.

Quickly turning away so she wouldn't be caught staring, Jude had swung around on her stool and faced forward. She might have felt a little instant attraction, but quickly formed the impression that she was not his type, nor he hers. Which was all beside the point anyway, since they were here to learn to cook, not to make a hookup. And just where had that thought, that word in particular come from? Jude admonished herself. It really wasn't like her at all. Normally she didn't have much reaction to strangers and definitely not this sort of visceral response. It threw her off. Made her feel unsure of herself, which always brought out her reserved side.

Jake, on the other hand, had no such compunctions about checking out his fellow students. To give him credit though, he had smiled just as widely at the two friends who were at least twice his age as he had at Jude.

Wondered briefly if he had already done something to make the lady sitting beside him dislike him. She certainly hadn't looked into his face for more than a moment. Though he'd managed a good look at hers. Pretty brown eyes, skin the color of warm cream, a wide mouth. She had long legs that went on forever, he noticed as he glanced down. He was a sucker for good legs. Grinning, he'd swiveled around to face Sylvia. This cooking class might just be the best idea his Mom had suggested in a long time. Prompted of course because the last time she'd been to visit he'd served delivery pizza. Though he ought to get points for that salad. Today he was going to learn how to make homemade corn tortillas with fresh vegetables, Pico de gallo, and guacamole. That didn't sound too complicated. His Mom would be so impressed.

Or so he's thought except that his tortillas kept falling apart in the skillet. And why was that when the pretty woman next to him, he'd learned her name was Jude, did not seem to have the same issue. Her tortillas held together perfectly. They'd mixed the masa flour with water, a tiny bit of oil, salt, and the fresh corn they'd stripped from the cob after boiling. Patting it into a ball, then flattening it to the width of the corn kernels with a plate, his had stuck first to the plate and then to his hands when he tried to transfer them to the hot oil in the skillet. And had broken into several pieces when he had tried to flip them over with a spatula. No one else seemed to be having these issues. Finally taking pity on the man, Jude had leaned over and whispered "you need to let them sit in the skillet longer before trying to flip them. Let them get a good brown crust on them first and then when you flip them, they'll stay together. Try that with your next one." Flashing her a smile he'd responded "Hey, thanks," and then "I was wondering if you were going to ignore me for the whole class." Turning a little pink, for she had in truth been trying to ignore him, though not for any reason he was thinking, Jude had offered a weak smile and turned back to the instructor who was giving instructions on knife skills while chopping onions for the pico de gallo. If her pulse had raced just a little at his smile, she did her best to cover it. As for his part, Jake couldn't figure out what he had done to turn her off. But never one to turn down a challenge, wasn't that why he was in this cooking class to begin with, he determined to work a little harder to get her to open up. The classes ran a series of six weeks, surely he could get her to like him at least a little bit in that amount of time.

It was the *bat.* He'd known it the first moment he had woken up the next morning. Even before his eyes had opened. He'd forgotten, had left the bat. There, on the sidewalk. *How could he be so stupid?* Nothing like this had ever happened to him before. He was always so careful. He knew exactly where it had landed, in the recessed doorway off the sidewalk that led into the storefront. He could imagine hearing it land there. When the old whore had moved to get away from him, it had thrown off his plan. Changed the way he had imagined it. She'd forced him to hurry, to modify his plan on the fly. Even though upset, he giggled again, couldn't stop himself at the thought *on the fly. Like all the flies that had been circling her stinking belongings.* He'd been so intent on getting away as soon as possible, on not being seen, that he'd forgotten to pick it up and take it. Well, there was nothing for it now, he couldn't go back, couldn't go near that area. They'd be watching, the cops. He'd finally calmed his breathing after several minutes, took a hot shower to calm down. It would be OK. They wouldn't find any fingerprints on the bat. He'd been wearing gloves when he'd bought it, the salesclerk hadn't thought anything about it since it was cold that day. He remembered it had been a stupid young kid, probably no more than twenty years old anyway. Kids today couldn't remember anything beyond where their phones were. He'd worn gloves too when he'd killed her. So, no fingerprints. They weren't in any database anyway. So, nothing to worry about. So what if they had the bat. It didn't tell them anything. He'd watched every newscast, listened to the radio in his car, for days. Listened for any story, any information about the homeless woman who had been killed downtown. He knew they probably wouldn't mention the bat, that was just the kind of detail they kept close during investigations. But there hadn't been a news story at all. He'd even gone so far as to pick up a copy of The Des Moines Register at the newspaper stand at the end of the block where he worked. Nothing there either. Just as he'd suspected, no one cared about some homeless whore. Still, the whole thing with the bat bothered him. It was a blemish on his perfect record. Not a serious one, not serious enough to get him caught, but still. He'd have to be more careful next time. Make sure his head was in the game. *In the game.* Baseball bat. The play on words struck him as funny, so funny, it had him mumbling repeatedly *in the game in the game in the game in the* out loud at his desk later that morning. He didn't notice the strange look cast his way by the man who'd walked by his open door just at that time.

Five months after his retirement, Art Kincaid was bored to tears. He just couldn't bring himself to commit or even enjoy any of the hobbies that had been suggested by all the well-wishers, fellow officers already retired. Woodworking was an absolute joke, cutting and even carving the simple shapes wasn't bad, but he'd quickly gotten frustrated using the teeny tiny sanding tool on his drill for the fine details, *who could stand to do this every day?* He'd tried fishing too, having every opportunity since there was so much coastline to Rhode Island, and remembering that it was something he had liked as a kid. But all that solitude, that quiet, just gave him too much time to think. And those fellow officers yet to retire thought he was living the high life. That everything was so wonderful for him now. They didn't want to believe any differently, because then they might have to consider what their own future retirement days might be like. It was hard, that's what it was like. Maybe even harder than the job had been. Praised and recognized for years of faithful service, he had nonetheless felt a failure. All because of the murders, the murders he had been sure were the work of a serial killer. But all his theories had led nowhere. The murders seemed to have stopped which, absolutely, was a blessing to his mind. If there had been a serial killer he seemed to have gone to ground. Maybe he'd died. Or ended up in prison for some other charge. Art watched the news daily, always expecting to hear of another murder. He knew his friends still on the Force would have let him know is there had been a break in any of the cases. Four months after retirement, he had gotten out of bed late one morning with a hell of a hangover, to find his wife Maureen waiting for him at the kitchen table. She'd looked angry, he'd seen that look before, and just really wasn't in the mood to deal with it this morning. Prepared for the fight, he'd been surprised then when she'd broken down with her hands over her face and cried uncontrollably. "Oh Honey, Honey. Now stop that. Whatever is wrong, I can fix it. Talk to me but please, please, stop crying. You know I've never been able to stand it when you cry." After a few moments to pull herself together, Maureen had looked up at her husband of more than forty years and told him "Art, you know I love you. I would have thought, if it was going to happen, that you would have started drinking years ago while on the Force, not now, after that stress had been lifted from your shoulders. I haven't, we haven't, worked this hard to lose everything. You won't even talk to me. You just go into your office at night and drink, alone. It's killing you, literally, and I just don't think I can stand by and watch it happen. You have to stop." After a few seconds of quivering lips, she'd continued "And Art, if you can't or won't stop, then I have to go. I cannot watch you destroy yourself. I will not. I'm not trying to give you an ultimatum, that isn't what this is. You know I love you," she'd said for the second time, "but I cannot live this way." Shocked, Art had started to protest, to say that everything would be fine. But he owed her more honesty than that. So, he'd sat holding the cup of coffee she'd made for him, collecting his thoughts. "Mo, I love you too. I didn't realize it was that bad. Maybe I didn't want to realize. Didn't want to see it was affecting you too. I don't want to lose you, I'll do anything to keep from losing you. I'll go for counseling, I promise. I saw too many other fellow officers who couldn't handle the same thing alone, sometimes counseling helped and sometimes it didn't. I'll stop, I make you that promise, but the counseling will just be like an insurance policy. And I'll talk to you more, tell you how I'm feeling, what I'm keeping balled up inside. I always did that, always told you about the cases even though we weren't supposed to. I didn't mean to stop, it just felt like I should have been happier, being retired, you know? Everything should have been perfect. Except it wasn't." "It is that serial killer case you were working last year, isn't it?" Maureen had been perceptive. "Yes, I admit it is. I just can't let go of it. It's not that I can't admit I was wrong, Mo. But I just still feel in my gut that I was right. That we should have been able to solve those murders. You know I always felt that the victims deserved justice, that the families deserved closure. I hate it that there were those that we didn't solve. And I guess I let it eat at me too much. Maybe the extra time I had since retiring just gave me more time to dwell on it." Relieved that, at last, he was opening up to her, Maureen had reached across the table, taken his hand in hers, "OK, Art, so where do we go from here? The fact is that those cases weren't solved. And I hate to be harsh, but they probably won't be. The question is, can you learn to live with that? Without becoming an alcoholic?" She'd searched his eyes then, he knew she'd know if he wasn't being honest. She always knew. "I'll have to, Mo. I'll just have to. I'm not saying it'll be easy, because I know it won't, but I won't lose you over this. I won't let it ruin my life, what we have."

He hadn't attended any of the meetings. Really hadn't credited the group as anything other than a bunch of losers with nothing better to do. But with time on his hands and that driving need to solve the cases, former Police Officer Art Kincaid decided to attend the next gathering of the group that called themselves "The Crime Solvers." A group of amateur detectives that seemed to have fixated on the murder cases announced a little over a year ago as serial killings. But then, wasn't he too fixated on them? He hadn't taken even a single drink since promising Maureen that he wouldn't, although the temptation was still there. That alone scared him. He'd been invited before, of course, the group would have loved having one of the officers who had worked the cases in their group, or even just to be at one of the meetings. Like a guest speaker. But he had always declined. Until now. He knew they met monthly. Knew too the names of the regular members because he had looked into their backgrounds at the beginning, just paranoid enough to consider that one of them could be the killer. The background checks had come out clean, most of them hadn't had even so much as a parking ticket. *Wannabe* cops had been his first thought.

But as he'd walked up to the picnic table set up under the pavilion in the park, that hadn't been his first impression. The group sat together, papers spread out on the table, held down by rocks to keep them from blowing away in the wind. Four men and two women. Most were middle-aged, over forty he would estimate. One guy was younger, probably early thirties. One of the women was older, likely in her late fifties. They didn't smile as he approached, just watched him until he was at the table. They'd known who he was, of course. But if there was any excitement running through the group, it was undetectable to Art. "Good afternoon," Art had nodded to the group in general, searching each face one at a time for any telltale signs of…of what? These people weren't the murderer, he really was getting paranoid he told himself. Need to get a grip. "Officer Kincaid," the elder of the men had stood and extended his hand to Art, "it's nice to meet you. I can speak for the group when I say that we are honored to have you join us today." *Honored,* Art had thought that was laying it on a little thick but chose to let it go. "Thank you. I'm glad to be here. Please go ahead with your meeting as you normally would, don't let me interrupt or get in the way." "That's fine, fine," the older man had said as he sat back down, "but first, let us introduce ourselves to you. We're an informal group, free flowing thoughts and brainstorming are always welcomed. My name is Jim Fredericks. I worked as a bank teller for almost forty-one years before retiring. Was on the receiving end of one of those *don't say anything and hand over the money from the register* kind of notes passed to me through the glass. Guy was hyped up on more than just adrenaline, I can tell you. Not real smart either, everything was videotaped, and the police met him just outside the door. They'd been tipped off when I pressed the little button just for that purpose under the counter. I guess you could say this has become my 'hobby' of sorts since I retired." And then the man sitting beside Jim had stood, shook hands, "And I'm Alfred, but my friends call me Al. Not to be confused with the Paul Simon song," he'd tried a little levity, getting only the tiniest of smiles from the policeman. "Unlike Jim, I'm still one of the everyday working stiffs. I work at the manufacturing plant out on Garrett Road. It's a pretty boring job. Mindless really on the assembly line." he shrugged, "so I guess that trying to solve these murders gives my brain some exercise." The woman who sat at the end of the bench next introduced herself, "It's nice to meet you. My name is Ann North.

I'm Jim's sister. Listening to him talk about this group, how exciting it was, got me hooked. I let him talk me into coming one day and I've been here ever since. And this," she'd gestured to the woman sitting directly across from her, "is my friend Kathy. We've been friends so long it just didn't feel right to do this without her, so I brought her in." Kathy had smiled at Art but didn't add to her friend's comments. Next to Kathy sat the youngest of the group, a thin man with the kind of facial scars that came from years of acne. "I'm Todd," the young man said stood quickly, as though it had been a belated thought. Extended his hand to Art. "Todd Thomas. I deliver mail on the east side of town. Got interested in this because a few of the murders were in my area. Heard lots of my customers talking about the crimes. Thought maybe I could help figure this out. I was familiar with the area of course. And knew all the people who lived there. I'd even delivered mail to one of the victims, the older lady they'd found in that park." It seemed to Art that Todd seemed to think that just because he had a dubious connection and was familiar with that area it gave him some sort of insight or insider information that the others didn't have. That the police didn't have. Of all of them, Art liked Todd the least on first impression. He seemed to fit the geeky, dull image Art had formed in his mind of the people who would meet week after week to talk about serial killings. After a glance at Todd as he'd sat back down, a glance that held more than just a little pity, the last man at the table had stood, "My name is Les, Les Grant. I'm retired too, like Jim. I used to be a schoolteacher. Taught Junior High science for most of my career. Always had a special interest in forensics."

After three classes, Jude found herself grinding her teeth, all because of the man sitting next to her. He just would not give up. After she had turned him down when he'd asked her if she'd like to have a coffee with him after the first class, he had nonetheless continued to try to gain her attention. One minute she'd be thinking that she was overreacting and that he was just a friendly guy and the next minute she'd been sure she'd caught him checking her out. Again. He was appealing, she'd give him points for that. Often caught off guard by his quick easy smile, she found herself smiling back before she stopped herself. And he didn't take himself too seriously, being the first one to make fun of himself when something they were cooking didn't turn out. Which was most of the time. More than once Sylvia had marveled at what a poor cook the man was, could anyone really be that bad? But she had realized soon enough that, at least some of the time, he was intentionally sabotaging his recipes just to get Jude to help him. Smiling to herself, it hadn't been the first time and likely not the last that there had been romance in one of her classes.

Jude was pleased with her Coq au Vin, scalloped potatoes, and braised brussels sprouts with the balsamic reduction. It looked great and had tasted even better. She was definitely making this for Sam and Carrie next time. They'd be blown away. Though the same couldn't be said for Jake's attempt. The main dish had looked more like a mush and the brussels sprouts were on the burnt side. Enough so that the whole kitchen area smelled like burnt cabbage. Unable to restrain herself, Jude had just stared at him with her nose crinkled up. Really, how could he be that bad of a cook? Sylvia explained everything perfectly. Sharing the meal she had cooked with him, because his own certainly wasn't edible, Jude found herself letting down her barriers, just a little. Just enough, he'd thought. He just needed an opening. He'd learned already that charm was wasted on her, she seemed to have no threshold for b.s. Which was actually something he admired, because he didn't like fake people either. So, he'd opted for honesty and friendliness, not a strong come on. He'd known instinctively that this was going to be a slow process. She was not an easy conquest, had more class than that. And as they'd gotten to know each other better, he'd been surprised to learn that he would be happy with her friendship, even if it never became anything more.

It was sparkling. There was no other way to describe it. The air was sparkling. The morning news weatherman had a technical term for it, explained that the temperature was balancing exactly at the pivot point to create the light floating ice crystals in the air. For the first time in a really long time, maybe in *forever*, Carrie felt happy. She loved Sam, was even confident that he loved her. She loved her job. Loved her little house. She had a new friend, one that promised to be a life-long friend. She'd never had one of those before. Normally not a fan of the cold, the magic of that mid-December day wasn't wasted on her. She'd run back inside, finding Sam already working at his computer, a relatively new change his employer had taken in response to the Covid outbreak. He'd easily transitioned to working remotely, since his job was working with computer programs. She'd called out to him from inside the door, not removing her thick mittens, scarf, or coat, "Sam, Sam, come here. You've got to see this. It's sparkling!" "What?" Sam asked as he maneuvered into the kitchen. One of the things Carrie had liked best when she'd toured the little house was the accessibility it gave Sam. There were no stairs, no thresholds between rooms, even the kitchen was wide enough to allow him to move freely. Which was good because she liked having him there with her when she cooked. She waited until he was at the door, then flung it open wide, "Look. Look, Sam. It's sparkling!"   Laughing, because it was indeed sparkling, Sam took her hand and tugged her down for a kiss. One that lingered. Had her lingering. As she'd walked back out again, into the sparkling air, she'd thought that really her life couldn't get any better. There were days when the dark clouds, the memories from her past, would invade, but today wasn't one of them. Those days were growing fewer and fewer. As were the nightmares.

Catching Jude just inside the front door, recognizing her tall, slender frame even in the padded down coat, Carrie asked her friend "Do you have plans for Saturday? I've been a terrible procrastinator and haven't bought the first Christmas present. I haven't even decorated the house. I didn't think I was going to, it's the taking down that I despise. So last year I didn't even do a tree. But this morning I suddenly feel like going all in. A tree, wreath for the front door, the whole bit. I want some of those big fat bulbs in the multi-colors, just like when I was a kid." She stopped then, stopped talking and stopped walking. Innocently enough, the memory of Christmas when she was just a child brought along with it other memories. These not nearly so nice. Seeing the odd look on her friend's face, Jude stopped too. "What is it, Carrie?" Shaking it off, she would not allow this to happen again, Carrie started walking again. "Oh, it was nothing. So, what about Saturday? Would you like a day of shopping? I know your tree is already up, saw it when you had us over last week. It's beautiful. You really lucked out when you found that condo. I love what you did out on your roof area, even though nothing is growing now, you still made it beautiful with all the tiny white fairy lights strung everywhere. It could be an all day excursion, I'll warn you, since I need to buy presents and holiday decorations too. There's that new restaurant I've been wanting to try too, I thought maybe we'd go for lunch." Growing warm inside the lobby with all her winter layers, Jude started peeling them off one at a time as they waited on the elevator. "I think that's a great idea. I think I'm done decorating, but I do need to pick up more gifts. I was thinking I'd like to get something for Kate. Although I have no idea what. Would you want to go in with me, get her something from both of us, together?" "Oh, yes, that's a great idea. Although I don't know what to get her either. Maybe inspiration will strike on Saturday. I need to pick up a few more things for Sam too. He's so hard to buy for. Says he doesn't need anything. Actually, he usually says that I am the only present he needs." "Aw, that's really romantic, Carrie. You're so lucky" Jude commented with a smile. "I know, right? That's why I want to find something really special for him. We usually exchange one big present and then fill stockings with silly little gifts. Last year he gave me a hand-painted scarf with penguins on it. I love it, it's so cute. I filled his with some silly bookmarks, new grill seasonings and some 'manly' earmuffs since he complained that the only ones he could find in the stores looked like they belonged on a twelve-year-old girl. I've been thinking, since he's working from home all the time now, about surprising him with a kitten. To keep him company during the day while I'm at work. I thought about a puppy, but there's so much work involved with new puppies. A kitten would be easier. For him, and for me. I'm not sure if he's a 'cat-kind-of-guy' but it's certainly one way to find out." Laughing, knowing that Sam would accept a bobcat if Carrie gave it to him, Jude suggested, "You could get a little stuffed animal kitten, put it in his stocking. He'd sure be confused when he pulled that out! Then bring in the real kitten. I think he'd love it, Carrie." "Good, I'm glad you don't think I'm nuts for thinking of a kitten as a gift for him. When it gets closer, I plan to visit the shelter, they always have a surplus of kittens. I'll even let him name it." They'd continued talking about the kitten, their Christmas plans during the ride up to their floor, finally setting a time on Saturday for Carrie to pick up Jude at her condo.

Kate had noticed that both of the girls seemed a little happier when they came to work lately. Not that either one had been the glum sort to start with. But Carrie seemed to have opened up more since making her new friend. And while she wasn't sure why, Jude seemed a little softer, a little prettier than usual over the past few weeks. These two were definitely some of Kate's favorites. She usually always favored the girls, although there had been a few men over the years that she had admired. One a very long time ago that she had taken under her wing. He never failed to send her flowers on Mother's Day even though he was now a busy executive. And wasn't that just the sweetest thing? There had been a few over the years, too, that Kate had disliked. Sometimes word would get out, as it always seemed to, about something unsavory from the past. Or something unethical they were doing presently. She really could not abide dishonesty. Saw no purpose to it. Some she spotted quickly as being pretentious, wearing their Rolex watches that she knew had cost too much money, all in an attempt to emulate the upper management of the company. They talked about their latest golf score loudly enough for everyone to hear. Trying to be impressive. Kate was not impressed. Although the man who had just come through the doors and headed to the elevator didn't fit into that category, there was just something about him that Kate could not warm up to. He was never mouthy, in fact he never said anything at all. Maybe that was why she just felt something off about him. Shyness was something she didn't mind, but something about the way he watched the others, especially the women, made her wary of him. She was glad that neither of the young women she liked so well had taken up with him. He'd been working there a couple of years, had a good attendance record. Truthfully, he was probably there more than Kate herself was, and that was saying something. But it didn't improve the uneasy feeling she had about the man.

Why was she always watching him? That old biddy at the front desk. *She should have been put out to pasture a long time ago,* he'd thought. Always looking down her nose at him. Probably still working well past her retirement age because she had wasted all her money. Oh, how he would have liked to make plans for her. Retirement plans, *permanent* retirement plans. But he was back to being cautious again, that mistake with the bat had made him sharpen up. Realign himself to his best skills. He could not make another mistake.

He'd first noticed the woman at the fast-food drive-through. It had only been a few weeks since the homeless woman, normally he would have allowed more time. But he couldn't waste time. There were too many of them. Too many whores. He'd noticed them before, of course he had, but he'd only recently started to realize the scope. Of his mission. That was how he thought of it. Normally manned by teenagers who couldn't get an order right if their lives depended on it, he'd noticed the woman in her fifties on more than one occasion. She was always polite when taking his money but clearly already focusing on the next order. Not really paying him any attention at all. Which was what he wanted, but it irked him anyway. You'd think she would be interested in him. Clearly, he was a step up from whatever she was coming from. And it was that lack of interest that made him so angry. Angry enough to make a spontaneous decision. He'd gone through the drive-through late one evening, less than ten minutes before closing time, knowing that would have to irritate everyone working inside. Knowing too that the burger he would receive would be the last leftover of the day. Maybe she wanted to take that burger home herself, he'd thought with a grin. *Well, that was just too bad, wasn't it?* He'd pulled over into the parking lot, appearing to be eating his meal, when she'd left work. She drove an older white van that had a few dents and was missing one hubcap. Slowly he'd followed her about a mile from the restaurant, watched her pull into a run-down apartment complex. Not the safest looking place, he'd thought. And had giggled. Not safe. "No place in the city is safe," he'd boasted out loud, not when he was living there. And another giggle had escaped. He'd watched to see which door she had entered, noted that it was a main door and caught a glimpse of her walking up a flight of stairs inside. So, not a first-floor apartment. That might have been just a little too convenient. It would take more watching, more planning, but he knew he'd succeed.

He'd made an appointment three weeks later with the manager of the apartment complex. Claimed that he was interested in renting an apartment there. Normally he didn't like to interact with others when he was *working* but he hadn't thought of any other way to gain information. Following the whore for weeks hadn't given him much to go on. Unlike most people, she didn't hold to a strict routine. Even her work schedule seemed to bounce around which, he assumed, was to be expected at a job like that. Depending on her work hours any given day, she'd run errands after work. Sometimes she would go to a movie at night or meet up with other people at a bar. A *bar.* Yes, she was definitely a whore. Decent women didn't go to bars. Mom had certainly never been in a bar in her whole life. Her short life. So, he'd met with the complex manager on a Wednesday afternoon, asked to be shown the available apartments. "They're pretty much all the same" he had been told but had insisted on seeing them all. One was on the ground floor, *God, it was pathetic.* Old brown carpeting that gave off a musty smell, a hole in the drywall where the doorknob had hit the wall. A tiny kitchen. No way would he ever eat anything that came out of that refrigerator. "Maybe there was something available on another floor," he'd suggested. He'd been shown two other units, one on the second floor and one on the fourth floor. The second-floor apartment had reeked of pet urine, enough so that his nausea must have been obvious to the building manager because he'd moved him on out of that apartment and on to the next pretty quickly. They really were all pretty much the same. *Disgusting.* Each floor seemed to be set up the same way, with apartment doors facing each other across a narrow hall. He'd counted four doors on each side of the hall, so eight apartments per floor. This wasn't giving him much information, but it was something. Thinking he'd have to continue his surveillance, he'd been thrilled as they'd left the final apartment to see the woman climbing the stairs. He'd made a pretense of standing aside so she could get by with her bags of groceries, all the while watching carefully to see which door she unlocked and entered. Apartment Number 29. Thinking he was still leading the manager to think he was really interested in an apartment, he'd continued asking questions as they went down the steps. Questions about security, what this part of town was like, what restaurants were close by, how the mail was delivered. The manager couldn't quite figure this guy out. He had seen the look on his face when he'd been shown the apartments, clearly, he had turned his nose up. It was true that the apartments weren't the best, but what did he expect for the rent? The manager had shown him the mail room for the tenants. Odd guy, the manager had thought again, he seemed really interested in the mail. Probably got a welfare check like some of his other tenants and wanted to make sure it would be delivered safely and on time. That he could understand. Little did he know that the man was paying close attention, *Number 27, Number 28, Number 29…B. Turner. B could be Barb or Beth or Brenda. Hmmm, wouldn't that be funny if he had two Brendas?* The thought made him giggle, earning a concerned look from the apartment manager, which he didn't even notice. Telling the manager that he would be back in touch if he decided to take one of the units, he'd left feeling very accomplished. He knew where she lived, and he knew at least her last name. The manager knew he'd never hear from the guy again, considered the last hour a waste of time although it did get him out of doing paperwork and was a good excuse for not calling the maintenance guy to deal with the toilet in Number 7. Why was it always a toilet?

Another stop at the fast-food restaurant later that week for lunch, when he knew she was working, had given him even more information. Her maroon nametag which he previously hadn't noticed said *Becky. Becky Turner. What a perfectly boring name for a whore.* Pulling away from the drive-thru, his mind raced with different scenarios. How best to do it? He had to be careful because she did seem to have some friends or family that she met up with occasionally. He needed to make sure she would be alone. And it couldn't be done at her apartment because it was on the fourth floor and because he couldn't risk the manager recognizing him. Following her after work later that week, at a safe distance so she wouldn't notice, his luck turned for the better. Steam had started coming from under the hood of her van and she pulled over into the parking lot of a nearby empty strip mall. The only windows not broken or boarded up were to a Chinese restaurant with only one car in front. He'd pulled in beside the car, knowing that she could see him, went inside the restaurant and placed a quick order for something he saw behind the counter. It really didn't matter what. Something he would throw away later. He left carrying a flat Styrofoam takeout tray within seven minutes of arriving. She had noticed the man, thought he looked a little familiar, but then, when you worked fast food, everyone looked familiar. Well, she didn't have many options. Waving at him as he'd started to drive past her van, she'd asked if he could help her after he rolled down his window. *Oh, he could help her alright.* Could he ever.

She had no idea how it had happened. Somehow, without her even being aware of it, she was dating a man. *She was dating Jake.* There was no other way to describe it. It had started out simply enough with coffee at a cafe after class. He'd carried most of the conversation. Had tried to draw her out of her shell. Getting nowhere, he'd tried a different tactic. "So, tell me, what's your fetish?" he'd asked with a feigned looked of innocence. Jude had choked, spit out the drink of coffee she had just taken. Laughing now, he'd said "Just kidding. Really, I'm just kidding. I just wanted to see if I could get a reaction from you." He'd made her laugh. He hadn't tried to cross any of her boundaries, maybe that was why Jude was caught off guard. They were just being friends. After the cooking classes had ended, he'd insisted on taking them all out for dinner, even Sylvia. Now that certainly couldn't be considered a date, not with three other women along. They'd met at a trendy restaurant for dinner one night when he'd mentioned that an author he liked was going to be there for a reading. To Jude's surprise, it was an author she very much enjoyed. Actually, she devoured every work by that author as soon as they were published so, it was only natural to go with Jake. He'd developed a habit of calling her of an evening, when she could see the sun setting through the large glass windows of her condo.

Sometimes she'd just be winding down, maybe enjoying a glass of wine. Other times she'd have changed into her comfy clothes and was mentally preparing for the next day. Even if she had gone to bed, she'd find herself waiting for his call. He did most of the talking, from the mundane to the serious to the humorous. Slowly she had told him more of her life. They'd discussed childhoods and bucket lists. It was weird that she was so comfortable talking to him. When he'd asked her to go out for pizza one Friday after work, she might have felt a twinge of concern that it sounded like a date, but pizza had sounded really good and who wanted to ever eat pizza alone? He'd picked her up outside her building, but that didn't mean anything. They went for walks, tried different restaurants, had even gone to the latest movie. Sat together in a theater with a giant tub of extra buttered popcorn between them. Until one day Jude realized the truth. *She was dating Jake. Jake was dating her.* Had been, it would seem, for the past three months. Feeling panic start to set in, but also not set in because, well, it was Jake. Her friend. Her *sneaky* friend. He'd made sure she was comfortable with him, that she trusted him, he had become her friend first. *Sneaky bastard,* she'd thought before drifting off to sleep one night, but she'd fallen asleep with a grin on her face.

She'd decided to turn the tables on him that Sunday morning when they met, as planned, for coffee and donuts at a local bakery. As she reached for a second, she told herself she didn't need the calories, the *empty* calories, and the high, high amount of sugar, but donuts were her weakness. One of them anyway. Jake had noticed. He was amazed that Jude could put away more donuts than he could. Anything covered with icing or with filling stuffed in the middle. He might have to make a call to Sylvia, ask if she could teach him how to make pastries. It didn't have to be donuts, he'd watched Kate consume scones and croissants and coffee cake and creme horns – always for breakfast. She'd looked up from the Bismarck filled with Bavarian cream to catch him watching her with a wide grim. *Yes, it was definitely time to turn things around a little bit, point the magnifying glass at him* she decided. She knew that she was probably completely transparent about her feelings. She'd never mastered the skill of holding a blank face. What she needed to know were his true feelings. He hadn't pushed her, in any way. Which was puzzling. *Didn't all men push?* Still with a mouthful of dough, she mumbled something at him that sounded like "so mmremh oor tish?" Laughing, Jake sat there shaking his head, took another sip of coffee. She'd eventually swallowed, enough so that she could talk clearly, "I said, so, what's your fetish?" It caught him off guard, had him busting out with a laugh. The other patrons turned, some smiled at the couple obviously enjoying each other's company. Others frowned, wondering what the joke was.

Kate noticed Jude come in on Tuesday morning. Something about the woman seemed a little livelier than usual. She'd waved as she saw Carrie step into the elevator. "Carrie! Hey Carrie, hold it for me please." She'd rushed into the small box beside Carrie, there was only one other person inside. She didn't know his name, but she had seen him around. He moved to the back corner to let her step inside. Though he hadn't met her eyes. *Just shy* she'd thought for the briefest moment. Carrie was unusually quiet during their ride up to their floor. She had become quieter when spending time with Jude, after she'd become comfortable enough to be herself. But she was being especially quiet that morning, Jude noticed. Separating to go to their separate offices, Jude had asked "lunch at the usual time, Carrie?" It was at that point that Carrie has just started crying uncontrollably. Embarrassed, she'd tried to escape into her office and shut the door, but Jude wasn't going to let that happen. Normally she respected the privacy of others, but Carrie had become her friend and there were times when a friend had to step over boundaries. Jude had stepped into the tidy little office with the framed motivational posters on the walls. *Be The Bridge* one poster proclaimed beneath the photograph of a long bridge spanning a river. Another said *Teamwork* and showed a group of rowers in one of those punt boats making a smooth wave in a lake. *Focus* showed a sun setting on a deserted beach. Colorful and professional,

Jude didn't know why she hadn't thought to hang posters like that in her office. Instead, she had several landscapes she had picked up at a consignment shop that had just appealed to her. She hadn't been sure why. "Look, Carrie," she'd started, "I'm not going to pry but something is wrong. What can I do to help? I can just listen. Or, you know I'd do anything for you. Is it Sam? Did you have a fight with Sam?" Carrie managed to lift her head from the tissues, "Sam? No, no. Nothing is wrong with Sam. I managed to leave the house this morning without breaking down. I don't think he noticed anything. Although he probably knew. He knows what today is. What anniversary it is. Twenty years. I can't believe it's been twenty years." This had started the tears again. It took what must have been a solid ten minutes for Carrie to gain some measure of control, raising her head and staring at the ceiling. Taking deep breaths. And more deep breaths. Her hair had fallen out of the clip and her mascara had run. Knowing that her friend never left her house without makeup, Jude sat patiently, not pushing. Just letting Carrie cry as long as she needed to. But letting Carrie know she was there. Finally gaining some control, Carrie tried to make a joke about what a hot mess she must seem. "Don't, Carrie. Don't joke. You don't have to do that with me. Surely you know by now that you don't have to do that with me. Just tell me." And Carrie had. For only the second time in her life, she told someone else everything about that awful night. Twenty years ago. The words had been halting at first, jumbled as were her thoughts, she really didn't know how to tell the story. The real story. It might seem like a nightmare to her most of the time, and did occasionally surface in her nightmares, but she tried to tell herself it was just a story.

"I was eight years old," Carrie started. "Just eight years old. I lived in one of those perfect houses, white picket fence and a back yard. I was an only child. My parents were great. Like from one of those tv sitcoms, you know, only it was for real. My Dad drove a taxi. I know that sounds dumb, but it really was a pretty good job back then. That, plus the money Mom brought in from babysitting a few of the neighborhood kids, made it possible for them to afford the little house in the decent neighborhood. And there were always the kids Mom babysat at our house, so even though I was an only child I always had other kids around to play with. It was late summertime, hot and humid. It was dinnertime on a Friday night. Dad had made pork chops and baked potatoes on the grill, so it didn't heat up the house. He was famous for his pork chops." Another small sob had crept up then. After a few seconds she continued, "We had all just sat down to eat at the kitchen table when there was a knock on the front door. Dad answered it. There was some man there, he said his car had broken down and asked if he could use our phone. That was back before everyone carried cell phones, remember?"

Jude nodded but didn't break into Carrie's story. "Dad felt sorry for the guy, said 'Sure' and let him into the house. That's when the guy had pulled out a gun, told us all to shut up and to not make any trouble. That everything would be OK as long as we didn't make any trouble. Everything would be OK, he said. He told my Dad to give him his wallet, he took all the money out of it. I didn't understand what was happening, I think I was crying because he yelled for me to shut up. I remember Mom hushing me, saying everything was going to be OK, I just needed to stay quiet. He made my Dad sit back down at the table and while he held the gun on me, he made my Mom tie Dad's hands behind the chair with a cord of some kind the guy had in his back pocket. I could tell Mom didn't want to do it, but the guy said if she didn't do it, didn't tie it tight, that he would know and he would shoot me. After Dad was all tied up, the man made my Mom go upstairs, he said he wanted all her jewelry. Mom always wore the prettiest jewelry, although I realize now that most of it was costume jewelry. I remember big colorful crystal pins shaped like birds or snowflakes. It couldn't have been worth much. Dad told me to run, to go next door and tell our neighbors to get the police. To get away. But I was just crying and crying. We heard the sound of a gunshot and then the man came running back down the stairs. Jude, that sound is one I'll never forget. It was the sound of my Mom dying. By that time, my Dad had started to try to get loose, he was trying to fight the guy however he could even though he was still tied up. The man shot Daddy. I watched him when he shot my Daddy. Oh Jude, it was so horrible. I saw his face. The look on his face. How desperate do you have to be to shoot another human being? That's what I saw – desperation. I don't know why he didn't shoot me too, but he ran out the back door with the money from Dad's wallet and some of Mom's jewelry, I'll bet he didn't even get a hundred dollars' worth. Probably not even that. I don't know why he didn't shoot me. Later people said it was probably because he heard the sirens coming. I don't remember the sirens." She stopped then, a little surprised that she had told so much. Needing to finish it she continued, "so, I was raised by my grandparents. My Mom's parents. They were great, but really weren't equipped to handle a really disturbed little girl. Psychiatry wasn't much of a thing back then, at least not to their generation." Finally, she got the last of it out, "I didn't do anything, Jude. I didn't run for help. I didn't fight the guy. I didn't do anything but stand there and cry. I didn't even try to save them." Spent now, Carrie slumped back in her chair. "Carrie, oh Carrie," Jude took her friend's hands, "I don't even know what to say. I'm so so sorry that you had to go through that. No child should ever have to go through that. And it was twenty years ago today, you said?" After her friend shook her head in confirmation, Jude continued "I don't even know why you came in today, sweetie. You should have called in sick and stayed home, took care of yourself." "No, that would have made it worse," Carrie said, "although I'm not sure how I could be a worse mess than I am right now." Jude didn't know how to help her friend. She was so very unequipped to make things better for her. So she'd been surprised when Carrie had leaned forward and said simply "Thank you." Shocked, Jude had asked "Thank you? What for?" "Just for listening to me, for not judging me, for letting me tell the whole thing. Some people don't, you know. Not that I have tried to tell many people, especially not in recent years. When I was still young, they'd always stop me part-of-the-way through and tell me not to dwell on it. I didn't even know what that word meant. Other than Sam, you are the only person I've told the whole story to." Her friend looked drained. "OK, Carrie, so here's what we're going to do. I'm going to give you some space and time alone, about an hour, and I want you to dwell on it all you want. You need to *dwell* on it. When I come back, we'll fix your face and I'm taking you to lunch. We'll take the rest of the day off, both of us. We can play it however you want. We can hit the first bar we come to and drink ourselves silly. Or we can eat chocolate and shop all afternoon. Whatever makes you feel better." Jude handed the box of tissues to Carrie, gave her a gentle smile, "OK?" "Yes," Carrie agreed "that will be OK. Although we might hit that bar and then eat lots of chocolate and spend lots of money shopping, in that order." "Deal," Jude smiled as she shut Carrie's door behind her. Going into her own office and shutting the door, it had taken most of that hour for Jude herself to work through the emotions brought on by her friend's story. Roughly the same age as Carrie, she knew that those had been innocent times. And Carrie was only eight years old. Eight years old. So much made sense now. Like Carrie's timidity, her shyness. It was really so much more than that. It was self-protection. Self-preservation. Jude was honored that Carrie had shared such an intimate and private secret. She knew there wasn't much she could do for her, but she could certainly take this afternoon to try to put some salve on the wounds. Not knowing exactly who Carrie reported to, Jude had taken the elevator down to talk to Kate. Something must have shown on her face because Kate was immediately concerned when she'd walked up to the desk. "Jude, what's wrong? Are you sick?" Kate had asked. *How to do this?* Jude had thought before plunging in. "No, I'm not sick and Carrie isn't either. Well, not like you mean. She's really upset, and I need to get her out of here for the rest of the day. Both of us. I don't know who she reports to, can you help me get to the right person?" Seeing the seriousness on her face, Kate nodded "Don't you worry about it. I know who she reports to, and I know your supervisor too. I will talk to both of them. It'll be fine. Trust me, it'll be fine." And it had been. Though she already admired the older woman, in that moment she *appreciated* her. Kate hadn't asked questions, demanded an explanation. Somehow, she'd sensed and respected that whatever was wrong was Carrie's story to tell, or not to tell. Whatever Kate said or however she handled it, Jude and Carrie would never know, but they both took the afternoon away from work and it was never mentioned. Some of her anxiety had eased by the time Jude dropped her off at home, since Jude had decided that the two Tom Collins Carrie had consumed with lunch might have just been her friend's limit. Over her limit. She'd watched Carrie weave her way to the front door, saw Sam reach up and pull her into his lap as he was waiting in the open doorway. Jude had cautiously called him earlier while Carrie was using the bathroom in the mall, to let him know where they were and what was going on. Her friend would really be OK now, Jude knew. Sam would take care of her.

It was over dinner that Friday night when Jude had looked up to find Jake watching her intently. Blushing, she realized she hadn't been carrying on her side of a conversation, really hadn't even been paying attention to his. Her mind was still on Carrie and everything her friend had told her. "I'm sorry, Jake. I know I'm not all the way here. Do you just want to call it a night?" He'd reached across the table, taken her hand in his. "No, what I'd really like is to know what's bothering you." Tempted, Jude shook her head, "I can't. It isn't my story to tell." After a few moments, he nodded, just asking "Can I help?" That was all. Just like that. Jude realized once again that this man was special. He hadn't jumped to any conclusions. Hadn't pushed her to tell him what she knew. Hadn't demanded to know any details. He'd just accepted. Accepted and offered help. Focusing on him completely now, Jude answered, "You already have" and smiled into his eyes. He really had the most amazing blue eyes. "Ah, so I see you're back with me," he said. "Good, because I have something I want to ask you. Would you want to come with me tomorrow, I know it's short notice, to dinner at my folks' house? It's Dad's birthday and Mom's pulling out all the stops. She's horrible at keeping secrets, so I'm pretty sure Dad knows all about it. It'll just be Mom and Dad, me and you, and my three younger brothers. Just dinner and cake afterwards. It's OK if you don't want to, I'll understand." And she had almost said 'No,' just automatically. But she was learning that friendships and whatever this was with Jake, were special things and that she was so lucky to have both Carrie and Jake in her life. "That would be great. Except there's one problem. You are only giving me one day's notice to get your Dad a present." Smiling, Jake had assured her "Oh, you don't have to do that. It isn't expected. I think I may have just mentioned you to Mom and she wants to meet you." If she wasn't nervous before, now Jude was. This sounded an awful lot like 'meeting the parents.' But she was getting ahead of herself. "I didn't realize that you had three younger brothers. You've never said. What are they like?" And he'd made her laugh for the next hour as he'd told stories about growing up as the oldest of four, two of them twins.

He'd picked her up at eleven, had smiled when he'd seen the neatly wrapped package she brought to the car. Had noted and appreciated the jeans she wore as she'd walked down the sidewalk. He was used to her work 'uniform' and the occasional dress she wore out to dinner. This was the first time he'd seen her in jeans. And he had to admit that they looked really good on her. As she slid into the passenger seat, he'd picked up her perfume. He always loved the way she smelled. It was always the same, one of these days he would get around to asking the name. Most of the time it made him almost crazy with wanting her. In his parent's driveway, he'd moved around to open the door for Jude. Knowing full well that his brothers, and also likely his mother, were watching from windows in the house, he'd leaned it and just barely placed his lips on hers. A soft kiss. And for a few moments they'd just stayed there. It wasn't until his Dad had said it twice from the front door that Jake heard "Jacob, are you going to let that girl go already and come inside? You know the neighbors are probably watching." Jude had blushed and a big grin had spread across Jake's face. He did know that the neighbors were probably watching. His parents had lived in this same house for over thirty years and he and his brothers had grown up there. "Come on," Jake said, "We'd better go inside so I can introduce you around."

At the front door, Jude smiled at the man who was an older version of Jake. Same ice blue eyes, though there was a little gray in the hair. Good genes, she decided as Jake introduced them. "Jude, this is my Dad Ollie. Dad, this is Jude Anderson." She hadn't even thought about it, maybe because he looked so much like Jake, but Jude had bent forward and kissed Ollie on the cheek, handing him the wrapped box with the blue bow at the same time. "Happy Birthday, Mr. Barton." Pleased at the kiss, the genuineness of this girl, a girl that might just be right for his son, Ollie responded, "Now, none of that 'Mr.' stuff. It's Ollie to all my friends, and I'm sure we're going to be friends. Come on into the kitchen and meet Helen, the Saint who puts up with me and four rowdy sons." Smiling, Jude could just imagine the Jake had been a rowdy teenager, she'd stepped into a kitchen that smelled like heaven. She had no idea what was for dinner, but if it was half as good as it smelled, she was in for a treat. The petite woman with salt-and-pepper hair cut short turned with an easy smile, "Welcome, welcome, Jude. We're so glad you could come today. And look, how nice, you brought the birthday boy a gift. I do hope it isn't candy, his doctors are always telling him to lay off the candy. But that's like telling a fish not to get wet." It was then that Jake's three brothers had decided to make an entrance, "When are we eating, Mom? I'm starving." This had come from the tallest of the three, tallest but Jude was fairly certain not the oldest. "Bradley," his mother shook her head at him, "Can't you behave when we have company?" Grinning at Jude, he'd then made a show of leading her to a chair, pulling it out for her and, with a slight bow had sat beside her. "Hi, I'm Brad, in case you didn't get that from my Mom. I really do have good manners. Unlike my brother, he probably told you nothing about us. I'm the brilliant, charming, athletic one. It's so sad that I got all of the best traits and my brothers got none." He'd been wrong, Jake had told her quite a bit about each brother. So Jude knew even before his speech that Bradley was the typical class clown. Tall and awkward at only fourteen, he preferred to make people laugh more than anything. As Jake pulled the chair out on the other side of Jude, preparing the sit down, the swinging door into the kitchen flew open with a bang as two other copies of their father loudly joined the group. One of them, who Jude would learn was Adam, had quickly slipped into the chair Jake was holding, "Thanks, Bro."

Jude returned his grin as the last brother had taken the seat directly across from her. Were they her buffer, she'd wondered fleetingly? More likely they were her entertainment for the evening. As an only child herself, she'd always been jealous of big families, of the fun and affection they must have. Half-way through the meal, she revised her previous perception, it was more like a circus. She'd answered questions peppered at her from the boys on all sides. *Where was she from? What had been her favorite subject in school? Did she have any brothers or sisters? How had Jake gotten lucky enough to meet her? Did she like basketball? What was her favorite movie? Did she like to play video games? Could she cook? Did she have a job? Did she like it?* For the most part Helen had let it play out, finding she rather liked having her sons ask the questions. She could get some of the answers she wanted this way, without having to seem too pushy. Oh, they were always a lot to cope with, but her boys could come in useful sometimes. And she could observe. And listen. Jake had brought girlfriends and girl friends home before, although it had been a few years. But as much as he'd tried to downplay tonight's dinner, she'd know this one was special. A mother always knew. And since she thought each of her sons was perfect, in their own way, she'd watched how Jude handled their antics. She liked that she noticed the young woman's eyes sparkled when they landed on Jake. Liked too that she didn't take offense at any of his brothers' shenanigans. And when, after the meal was over, the girl had stood up and starting clearing dishes, she'd decided she liked her very much. She'd never forget the girl that their son Shawn had brought home that one time – she'd acted like a princess as she let everyone, including Shawn, wait on her. No, she decided that Jude wasn't like that. Before Jude could carry the first armload of dishes to the sink, Helen had stopped her "You just leave those right there. In this family, these boys here take turns with the dinner dishes. Since they do most of the eating, it's only fair that they do their share of the cleanup. You just stay right where you are," and she'd noticed with a slight smile that Jake had taken Jude's hand as she'd sat back down. "I know that Ollie can hardly wait to have his after-dinner coffee, but I have something else first. I hope you like sweets." She returned from the kitchen carrying a huge birthday cake covered in so many candles Jude worried about the smoke detector going off. Smiling at this amazing woman, Jude remembered "Oh! I almost forgot. Yes, I do love cake, but I almost forgot about Mr., um, Ollie's gift. You should open it now." When his mother had glanced at him, Jake had just shrugged. He really had no idea what was in the package, but he was dying to find out. Ollie was smiling even before the paper was off the box, "Oh, I can smell it already. Heaven. This is going to be heaven." Grinning proudly, he held up the malleable bag of coffee beans for Helen to see. "Oh, and it's a dark roast, my favorite kind. We'll just have a big slice of that cake and then you can go with me back to my 'espresso bar' in the living room and I'll show you how it's done." Jake leaned in, whispered loud enough for everyone to hear, "you've done it now, Jude. You won't escape until he's shown you how that fancy gadget of his works. Back in the day, there was a wet bar in the living room, it's of that era. But when they remodeled about seven years ago Dad converted it into what he calls his 'espresso bar.' He's an amateur barista now." Which was fine with Jude because drinking coffee was one of her favorite pastimes. She'd chosen that particular brand of coffee because it was one of her personal favorites. When they'd finally left for the evening, his brothers yelled out to Jake just as he shut the door on Jude's side of the car. He'd waved them to go back to their basketball game on the driveway, the old hoop still where it had been when he still lived at home. "Hey, man. Don't ignore us. We know you're too old to play against us young studs and we don't want to embarrass you in front of your girlfriend. But come over here a second." This had been from Bradley. Smiling weakly at Jude, Jake had motioned that he would be right back. "So, we made a decision," Shawn told his oldest brother, "and we decided to keep her." "What?" totally caught off guard, Jake had repeated the question. Had he heard correctly? "We've decided to keep her. So don't screw this up. Because if you do, we're keeping her and throwing you back." Thinking he was making a joke at first, Jake had looked at his three brothers, arms linked around each other's shoulders in unison, serious faces which were seldom serious, and realized that they really meant it. As a group, they had that same look that he called his Mom's 'no nonsense' look. Giving them a nod, also quite serious, he's answered "Well, it's a good thing I don't plan to screw it up, then, isn't it?" Mulling it over as he climbed into the car, he told Jude "I think, I'm not sure, but I think I was just asked what my intentions are?" "What?" surprise had her voice going up a notch, "your intentions? Towards me? That's what they asked you?" "Well, not in so many words, but yes. Basically, you're 'in' and I'm 'out' if I let you get away." Pleased, and little flattered, Jude smiled into his eyes, "Guess you'd better not let me get away then, had you?" She said it teasingly. Jake didn't want to scare her off by moving too fast, so he'd just smiled back, but his thoughts were already moving in that direction.

The group met on Friday that week in the conference room they had scheduled in the small community center in Pawtucket due to the forecast of rain. Always punctual, Art noted when he went through the swinging doors that everyone else was already at the table. They were all there, perfect attendance that afternoon. As he sat down, he noticed though that they all wore serious expressions. Not a smiling group today. It was Jim, their unofficial spokesman, who'd cleared his throat. "Officer Kincaid," he'd started when Art had interrupted him "It's Art, just Art now please." Nodding, Jim continued "Art, you've been coming to our sessions for some time now. We appreciate that. But we've noticed that, although you always listen carefully, you never contribute to the group. You never share your thoughts with us, only expecting we give you ours." He could have continued, making it more of an accusation, but he'd stopped speaking there, willing to let the silence stretch as long as necessary to get a response from the former policeman. *He'd have made a good interrogator,* Art thought to himself. Art sat, mulling over what had been said. After some time, on a sigh, he said "Fair enough. I guess I haven't contributed. Habit. Old habit. A hard one to break. Officers of the Law aren't allowed to talk about cases, not allowed to give details or discuss ongoing investigations. Not supposed to even talk to our spouses about sensitive or ongoing cases. Most don't discuss investigations even when they are past that stage when they're solved. I'm a bit like an old bulldog, it's a hard habit for me to give up." Kathy gave him a weak smile, nodding as though she understood. The others seemed to soften a little too, at Art's explanation. He continued "But, I can see your point too. While I can't disclose any confidential information to the group, because those deaths are still ongoing investigations, we never close an unsolved murder, I think I am free to talk about any information which was made public knowledge at the time." Al stood up then, he always stood up when he spoke, "I think we can live with those boundaries. More than anything, I think we'd like your thoughts, your feelings, about the information we've collected, the possibilities we've developed. If you think we're on course or off target. We spend an awful lot of time doing this, and it means something special to each one of us." So, for the rest of that afternoon session, which had stretched into the early evening, Art had joined the discussion. Pointed out a few, really just a few, errors with the maps the group had developed. When he'd questioned two hand-drawn marks on the map, Todd had spoken up, rather proudly, "I added those. They're alleys, but they don't go all the way through. I pass them on my mail route." Interested, Art noted "that's a good observation, Todd. This is the first time I've seen them on a map of the area." Though they had produced no suspects, he did listen and shared thoughts about the type of person who would be a serial killer. Driving home later, Art realized that he felt a little lighter after today's meeting. And that maybe he would get serious with this group and really try to solve this thing, *finally*. Maureen noticed when he came through the door that he seemed better. Better than he had been. The surprise flowers had meant a lot too, he hadn't done that in years. Happily placing them into a large glass in the center of the table, she found herself humming as she brought their supper to the table. For the first time in a while, she felt like maybe everything would be OK.

As Jude walked through the automatic door that Monday morning, she saw Carrie talking at the desk with Kate. Walking over, she removed two frappes from the carboard carrier that had been handed to her at the drive-thru window, sitting one on Kate's desk, handing one to Carrie, and keeping the other for herself. "Well isn't that just a beautiful thing," Kate smiled up from her chair at Jude, looking at the artistic beverage with whipped topping. "They say that a man can be bribed with money or sex, but if you want to bribe a woman, use chocolate." This made both women laugh as they started down the hall to the elevators. "She's amazing," Carrie commented as the doors opened and they stepped inside. Three other people were inside, all going up. Standing in the front, Carrie teased "So, how was your meet-the-parents dinner this weekend?" "Actually," Jude said, "it was really nice. They are a wonderful couple, the whole family is pretty fabulous. Jake's Dad has this fancy espresso machine set up and he had so much fun firing it up, frothing the milk for our after-dinner coffee. It was really good too. And his Mom is wonderful too. Just like you'd imagine for the mom of four boys. Four *rowdy* boys. I really liked them all. They made me feel comfortable and it really wasn't awkward at all." "Wow, you don't hear that very often," Carrie commented, "so, did it put you in the mood to hear wedding bells?" That earned her a *really* look as Jude raised her eyebrows, laughing. "To tell you the truth, that thought doesn't scare me as much as it once did. But, I've never really felt about anyone the way I feel about Jake. I'm always happy when I'm with him. I do know that. But we're taking it slow, marriage isn't something either one of us would jump into too quickly. I want to be sure. I'm sure he feels the same way. But OK, now that you brought it up, you're fair game. What about you and Sam? Any wedding bells there?" As they stopped at the third floor to let someone off the elevator, Carrie answered "No way. That isn't for me. Don't get me wrong, I love Sam, but I don't want the whole ceremony thing. Of course, the thought of standing up in front of a crowd in a big white dress scares the hell out of me. And I wouldn't want to put Sam through a ceremony in his wheelchair either. The first dance would be awkward for him." Privately Jude thought Carrie was selling Sam short but kept the thought to herself. "He hasn't ever asked?" "No, we talked about it once because he wanted to know how I felt about marriage. A long time ago. He agreed with me. We're good just like we are." This was said just as they stepped off onto their floor. Carrie had whispered then, "did you notice that guy in the elevator? The one who never talks? He was popping his knuckles over and over again, it was so loud. I think he's a strange one. No one even seems to know his name." Jude had glanced back over her shoulder just as the doors were closing, the look on the man's face was really disturbing. She had always thought him harmless, just a little strange, but the look on his face was one that made her want to run. Shaking her head because it had just been a quick glance as the doors shut and she was probably mistaken anyway, Jude headed into her office while Carrie opened the door across the hall.

He was seething. How dare that woman talk that way about marriage? The tall one was OK, he'd decided, at least she was moving in the right direction. Towards a husband and family. But the little one, clearly living with a man with no intention of marrying him, was completely different. Unacceptable. A whore. That demanded a response. She needed to be put in her place. And that place was *in the ground*. A guffaw escaped him at that thought as he stepped onto his own office floor. Now to make a plan. He already knew her name, had known it for some time. Carrie Sanders. It would be easy enough to find out where she lived, but since she lived with a man, he didn't want to take a chance of doing it at her home. He'd have to find another place. And she was always with that other woman, Jude was her name. It might be tricky to catch her alone. He'd have to study on it, come up with a solid plan. Anticipation building, he'd shut the door to his office. Didn't notice the woman several doors down who'd glanced into the hall at the sound of the slamming door.

It had taken weeks for an opportunity to arise. He'd been following her at a very careful distance after work, but he'd just not felt confident about a place or time to do it. She parked each day in the huge company parking garage, which might have been suitable, but there were always others coming and going at the same time. There was no guarantee that another vehicle wouldn't come up or down the spiral inside the garage at any given moment. It had been a Thursday when he'd followed her that she deviated from her route home. Her blinker had signaled, and she'd turned off the road at a Farmer's Market. Walking the aisles, she'd had her phone pressed to her ear. "OK, Sam, I'm here and looking. Tell me again what I'm after." After buying three packs of the fresh blueberries and the tomatoes Sam wanted, Carrie spontaneously also picked up a bag of the sweet corn at one table. It just looked too good to pass up. As she'd walked back to her car, to her surprise, she saw the familiar face of the strange man from work. She hadn't spoken first, had been surprised when the man had. Since he hadn't spoken to her the entire time they'd both worked at BICO. "Excuse me," he'd said, obviously upset, "I recognized you from work and I really could use some help. If you don't mind. My car is parked just a few rows over, it's over there," he'd pointed with his index finger to the last row. "I don't know how this happened, I'm always so careful. Somehow, I accidentally locked my car with Bernie inside." At this point, the man was almost wringing his hands in distress. "Bernie?" Carrie had asked. "Oh, yes, I'm sorry. Bernie is my dog. You see, I thought this market allowed you to bring a dog to the vendor's tables, so I brought Bernie along today for his walk. He doesn't get enough exercise. He's getting older now. I thought he might like it here, all the movement and excitement, you know?

Anyway, I somehow accidentally locked him inside, along with my cell phone and car keys. I'm so upset. What do I do? It's hot today and the window isn't cracked any. He won't be able to breathe. I have to get him out!" Carrie had become upset too, she'd heard too many news stories of pets that had died after being left inside a hot car. "It's OK," she said, "I have my cell phone, let's go check on Bernie and call the police or 9-1-1 or something. I'm not really sure who to call, but we'll get someone. If we have to, we'll break the car window," "Oh, thank you, thank you so much," the man said as he led the way to his car, the only car parked that far out.

She'd awoken in the dark. She couldn't see anything. It was pitch back. She'd screamed, panicked. *Where was she?* He could hear her, only very faintly, if he stood directly over that area of the basement, on the floor above. That was good. If he could barely hear her, when he was expecting it, was listening for it, no one from outside would be able to hear her. Maybe not for a tornado, but the back basement room was coming in handy. *Let her scream,* he'd thought. She deserved it. That and so much more. Her fear would surely grow, he thought, if he postponed things a little longer. He had made plans, plans to take Jared and James out for ice cream, saw no reason to cancel those plans. The whore wasn't going anywhere. She could wait for him.

Hours later he'd descended the steps. He knew she'd heard him insert the key into the lock. The light that flooded the room must have been blinding, making him giggle. He could see her, she couldn't see him, at least not at first. When Carrie's sight had adjusted, she saw the man from BICO, the man she often saw in the elevator or in the hallway, the man who had asked for her help at the Farmers' Market. Shaking, terrified, she'd stared at him, not daring to look away. "Welcome," he said. "Welcome Carrie Sanders. I hope you like your accommodations, since this is the last place you will ever see. You see, I know the truth about you." *He knows,* Carrie's mind was racing, *how does he know what happened to my parents, what happened to me when I was a child?* "Yes," he continued, "I know that you are a whore. Just like so many other women. You are living with a man, out of wedlock. You have no intention of ever correcting that situation, no intention of ever becoming a wife or a mother. All the things a woman is supposed to be. That's despicable! So, you must be punished, like all the other whores. But I think that first I will let you, *encourage* you, to think about your sins. A night or two here, in this room, in the dark, ought to make you realize what you've done wrong. But there will be no redemption for you, you can be certain of that. No, after you've recognized your failings, you will join all the other whores." He'd left, locking the door behind him, giggling uncontrollably as he climbed the steps.

Sam had called Jude at 6:30. "Jude, this is Sam. I'm sorry to bother you but Carrie hasn't made it home from work yet. Did you two by any chance do something together after work? I don't remember her telling me, and it isn't like her to be this late." Concerned, because this didn't sound like Carrie at all, Jude had answered, "No, no we didn't make plans after work. When she left, she commented that she was running to the Farmers' Market to pick up a few ingredients for you, but that's all." "Yes, I spoke to her while she was there. But I can't imagine her still being there this late. I think the vendor stalls close up before now. I think I'm going to call the police." "Yes, and I'll be right over, Sam" Jude promised. When she arrived, Sam had already placed the missing person report to the dispatcher. "They made the record, took down the information. I don't know what else to do. I feel so useless. Should we go out and look for her? Call the hospitals? You don't think she's had an accident, do you?" "Calm down, Sam," although she was feeling anything but calm herself. "I'll make the calls to the hospitals, though I suspect that is likely police protocol to contact them." Hours later, Carrie still had not returned. "Do you think the police are looking for her? I've heard before that they have to wait 24 hours. But they don't know Carrie. She wouldn't do this" Sam worried. "I don't know about that 24-hour thing, Sam. I think that was in the past and that they immediately put out a report now for missing people" Jude had tried to reassure him. The calls to the hospitals had turned up nothing, no unidentified woman matching Carrie's description. "I'm going to make one more call, Sam. I'm calling Kate." "Kate from work? The Kate that Carrie has mentioned a time or two? You think Carrie might be with her?" "No, no I don't, but Kate sees everything. She might have seen or noticed or heard something."

In the dark, Carrie was terrified. There was no light, nothing for her eyes to see. She could only imagine what this place was. Dark, and damp, and musty smelling. Musty like moldy, and that made her cringe. She was hungry. Or maybe it was just thirst, she wasn't sure anymore. Slowly her mind was working its way through the situation, the things that had happened. *What was he going to do to her?* She was as terrified as she'd been all those years ago, felt just as helpless. *Well I'm not helpless now,* she'd said quietly to herself. Somewhere inside her, an anger started to grow. *I'm not an eight-year-old little girl any longer. He has no idea what happened to me back then, has no idea how it changed me, how it made me into the person I am now. And the person I am now, though a hot mess most of the time, is also a grown woman who has learned to take some measures of safety in her life. All those classes in self-defense. Then, she'd even been afraid to take the classes, but was grateful now that she had. And I do not want to die. I won't.* Slowly, she eased her way around the room, using her hands as her eyes. Why he hadn't bound her, she couldn't imagine, but was grateful for it. She remembered how helpless her father had been when he'd been tied to the chair. *Stop it!* she told herself, *you have to concentrate. On the here and now.* She'd felt the consistent eight-by-sixteen inch grid covering the walls, knew it had to be concrete block by the rough surface. It was on all the walls. The only opening seemed to be the door. Which had absolutely no give when she tried pushing it. She found nothing in the room, nothing along the floor that would be able to help her. She had only herself.

Hours later, she heard the key turning in the lock. Preparing herself, knowing the light would blind her at first, she planned to allow one minute, no more. She knew she probably only had one chance. He'd entered the room with a sneer on his face, *how had she ever thought he was shy?* "Still here I see," he'd said on a giggle, "were you waiting for me? Waiting for your punishment? I think it's time…" he'd stopped mid-sentence when Carrie had launched herself at him. Though she had no weapon, she had her nails which she clawed down his face. She'd kicked him at the knees, with all her might, hadn't stopped pummeling him with her fists. She grabbed the keys from his hand, had stabbed them into his face, aiming for his eyes. Slammed the door where he was still standing into him full force. Now he was the one screaming in pain. She'd run past him, taking the steps two at a time. Though she heard him coming behind her, she didn't slow, headed straight to the door she could see at the front of the house, onto the porch, leaped over the stairs and out onto the sidewalk, screaming as loud as she could. He was screaming behind her, "You whore! You're a whore! You don't deserve to live." But he saw beyond her several people coming their way, probably brought by her shouting. *Damn the whore!* No time to kill her now, he had to get away. He'd turned, ran back through the house and through the door connecting to the garage, grabbed the spare car keys he kept on a nail there, started the car and flew from the driveway. He passed the police car going in the opposite direction, toward his house. Shocked, *how had they responded so fast? That was too close.*

Sam had received the call at 9:42 pm. Jude and Kate were sitting together on the couch, all three trying to do their best to hold it together. Hanging up, he'd started towards the door. "They have her. They got her. They didn't get him, but they got Carrie. She's safe. Well, she's alive and safe now. I need to get to the hospital. I need to see her." Stopping mid-way across the small living room, he'd turned back, moved quickly over to Kate, kissed her cheek. "Thank you, oh thank you. You've saved her life. Saved my Carrie. I'll never be able to thank you enough." "Nonsense," Kate patted Sam's shoulder, "I just had a strange gut feeling about Simon Krupp, he was always watching the women, always watching Carrie. And you too, Jude. It was nothing to give his name to the policeman who was here with you." "Sam, I'll drive you. Kate, you come too. None of us will get any rest until we see Carrie," Jude said. "I don't think you're in any condition to drive, Sam, as upset as you are. I'll drive your van since it is wheelchair equipped. Come on, let's go get our girl."

She had some scratches of her own. Might possibly have done some of the damage herself with the keys. But none of that mattered. She was free. She was away from that hideous man. And, though she was still processing it, she had saved herself. That was something she would be proud of, someday. But right now, all she wanted was to see Sam roll down the hospital hall towards her, which he did at breakneck speed. He'd grabbed her, pulled her to him, then stopped himself as he'd eased his hold, "Oh, I'm so sorry. Am I hurting you? How bad are you hurt? The policewoman who called said you had superficial injuries" Sam couldn't seem to stop himself from babbling. It was either that or start blubbering. Which might happen anyway. "Oh Carrie, I was so scared. So scared when you didn't come home. What happened? Can you tell me what happened? No, no, I'm sorry, not now, you shouldn't tell me right now. We just need to get you home where you're safe. You don't ever have to tell me if you don't want to." Carrie had placed her hands on either side of Sam's face to stop him, "Sam, it's OK. I'm OK. He didn't do anything to me, not the way you mean. I think he was going to kill me. I'm not sure if he was going to torment me more, but I think he definitely planned to kill me." She paused at the sound of pain that escaped Sam, found herself soothing him rather than the other way around. "Really, I'm OK." She looked up and saw Jude and Kate at the end of the hall, standing back to give the couple their space. With a weak, watery smile she motioned them forward. This was her family.

Later, after a shower and some soup, Sam thought soup healed everything, she'd heard the whole story. How Jude had called Kate and Kate had somehow immediately made a connection to the strange man who worked at BICO. When the police hadn't taken her very seriously, wrote down the name but obviously thought it would lead to nothing, Kate had shown her true power. She'd pulled out all the stops, had bullied and shamed the policeman, dropped the names of the high-ranking politicians she would be contacting, even used guilt by asking how the policeman would feel if this was his sister. Every trick she had up her sleeve was brought to bear. They'd searched the name Simon Krupp, had found no police record, but did note the last known address and promised to go check it out. After a stern look from Kate, the policeman had raised his hands "Honest, Ma'am. Honest, I am going there right now to check it out." He had been just two blocks away in his cruiser when the 9-1-1 call came through from a bystander, claiming a distraught and hysterical woman was claiming she had been held captive. Switching the siren and lights on, he'd arrived within minutes. The ambulance had arrived within five minutes.

As Art approached the picnic tables beneath the shelter in the park, carrying the huge pan of brownies Maureen had sent with him, he noticed that the group seemed to be a little more animated, even more so than usual. He had to admit, this unique group of people didn't give up. Ever. Before he'd even taken a seat at one of the tables, everyone had turned to him as Les started to speak. "So, we thought, well really it was Todd's idea, and we thought we'd see how you felt about it. We thought the group might take a field trip today, go visit the neighborhood of the house where Carlene Dreissen lived, and was found dead." Todd stood anxiously at the end of the table, barely able to contain his excitement as he'd picked up the thread, "it's the area on the map where I showed you one of those unmarked alleys the last time we met. I thought you'd like to see them." Certain it would lead to nothing, Art had hesitated. But then he'd changed his mind, "I think that's a fair idea. I haven't been back to that scene in over a year, it might be good for me to take another look." And, seeing the looks on their faces when he'd said that *he* wanted a second look, he'd quickly added "And, it might be good to have new sets of eyes – yours – take a look around. You might notice a detail that we'd taken for granted at the time." The group had smiled, Todd actually beaming, as they'd headed to the two of the largest vehicles. As Art directed, they hadn't parked at the house itself but had instead parked on a side street and walked the few blocks to the house. Art knew that Carlene's husband had moved after the death of his wife, but he still didn't want whoever lived there now to know what their group was doing. "I think it best," he'd said, "if we walk in two groups rather than in one large group. Six people walking together might look a little odd and I don't want to concern any of the neighbors. One group of four, followed several yards behind by a second set would look less suspicious. Ann had volunteered, "Kathy and I will hang back. Two women walking together would be pretty common." "Yes," Art agreed, "that's a good idea Ann. We'll walk by the house, don't stop or linger, don't stare. I don't want to be a harassment to the new owner." "Oh," Todd jumped in, "I can give you their names. I still deliver mail on this route, so I know the names of the people who moved in after Sam Dreissen moved out. He moved only three months after his wife was killed. Guess he just couldn't stand staying there any longer. I didn't know them – the Dreissens – because neither was ever home when I delivered the mail. But I have met the new owners Bill – William – Ashmore and Russell Brown. Bill works from home, so I've met him as he's walked out to get the mail a few times. He has some kind of computer job, gets a lot of packages." After they'd all walked beyond the house and the two women had caught up with the rest of the group at the corner beyond the next block, Art had turned to Todd, "now, can you show me where that alley is, the one you marked on the map? I didn't see it when we walked past. "Oh, you wouldn't," Todd was quick to add. "It isn't a full alley that would run behind all the houses, it doesn't run along the property of the house. It actually forms a T with that road just a half a block down from the house. It's there," he'd pointed behind them along the path they'd just walked. "And an average person wouldn't notice it because it's covered by trees. That line of trees planted there, along the Jamison's side yard. They planted it for privacy, they told me. These houses are a little close. It's grown up over the years so now it completely blocks the view of the house next door and is so close that it hides the alley. There's no sign or street name. It only runs the one block, between two houses." Interested, Art had followed Todd as he led the group into the alley, walked the short distance to its end. He knew that they hadn't noticed the alley during their investigation, something that embarrassed him because he thought they'd been thorough. To be fair, the alley didn't border the victim's house, but it was still something they should have looked at, made note of. No evidence to be found here now, so much time had passed, and any evidence that might have been here would certainly be contaminated now. Still, Art walked the length a second time, making mental notes. This would be a really good hiding place. Or an escape route, hidden by the privacy screen of trees. Perfect covering from any onlookers. And no home security cameras pointing down the alley. Jim, noting Art's sincere interest, spoke up, "I don't know if this would add any value, but if you like, I carry a metal detector in my car. I can walk back and get it." Art looked at Jim, *what kind of person carried a metal detector in his car?* Knowing exactly what Art was thinking, Jim grinned. "Yes, I am an amateur metal detectorist. One of those strange people you see out on beaches and other public places walking back-and-forth. I get a lot of strange looks, people wondering if I don't have anything else to do. Usually, I find coins and smashed soda cans, although about four years ago I did dig up a diamond ring out on Goosewing Beach. It took a little sleuthing on her part, but Ann found an old post on social media about a lost engagement ring in that area. We PM'd the owner and, after getting a good description, plus her engagement photo where she was wearing the ring, we returned the ring to her. It was pretty cool. She and her husband even had a second ceremony to renew their vows using the original ring." Ann commented "It was sweet. They even invited Jim and I to the ceremony, they had it right there on that same beach." With Jim running the detector, they covered the alley in a grid pattern, sweeping back and forth. Items uncovered included some loose change, one bottle cap, several rusted nails, but nothing that could plausibly be associated with the murder. Thinking back, Art recalled, the coroner report indicated that the victim was likely poisoned several hours before actual death, and her coworkers at the school indicated she went home early that day not feeling well. "It's very possible that the killer was never even in this area on that day. Somehow, he, or she, got to the victim while she was at work." Todd looked crestfallen that his idea had been a dead end, but Art had kindly encouraged him, telling him "it was a good idea, Todd. This area wasn't in any of the official reports. I'm going to pass it along to one of my buddies still on the force, have them update the file. Add it to the official maps, should it ever be needed for reference in the future. I know it's getting late today, but next week, let's try the same thing as today, only at the Martin Luther King Jr Elementary school where she worked. We can't enter the school or go on school grounds since we are not officially linked with the investigation in any way," he could see the looks of disappointment, "but there is a public park directly across the street. We can watch the routine of the school, see who comes and goes, and even run Jim's detector in the park."

She was tired of being watched. Being handled with kid gloves. Sam treated her like she was a fragile glass vase that might shatter if not carried gently. And Jude was just as bad. Calling her at least twice a day, to see *how she was doing?* Although she couldn't explain it, not even to herself, the anxieties and irrational fears from the past were falling away. Instead of growing, they had shrunk. Shrunk to a size so small, so small she hardly felt them anymore. She'd never forget the helplessness she'd felt as a child, had felt again so recently. But over the past few weeks, Carrie had started to feel other things too. Like pride. Pride that she had not been a victim, like so many others. Proud that she had fought back. And not just fought back, but she had *won*. She'd saved herself. She'd snapped at Sam just that morning, the morning of her first day back to work. He hadn't really done anything to deserve it, he was trying to take care of her. "Are you sure?" he'd asked as he'd handed her a small bag he'd packed. She looked inside, saw the apple and small container of peanut butter. She'd ignored his question, asked one of her own instead "What's this?" "Just a snack," he'd said. He'd never done that before, not *before*. And somehow it just really struck her the wrong way. She'd yelled at him. Actually yelled. For probably the first time in her life, she'd yelled in anger at another person. And it was at *Sam*. Sam, who she loved and who had been there for her every minute of the past few weeks. Even before that. She knew she was being irrational. She stomped her way to her car, had driven the distance to work, irritated the entire way. As she'd entered, Kate had motioned her over. When she'd approached the desk, Kate handed her, balanced on a small paper plate, a yellow cupcake with tiny candy stars. That moment was probably when it started. When she'd seen the concern, the caring on the face of the dear older woman. The woman who had helped in a very real way, to save her. The tears streamed down her face. "Oh, Honey," Kate started as she came around the desk to Carrie, "is it too soon? Too soon for you to come back to work? No one will say anything if you take more time." During the exchange, Jude had come from behind Carrie, gently wrapped her arms around her friend. "She's right, you know, Carrie. If you need more time, everyone will understand." "No, no, no, you don't understand," Carrie tried to talk through the tears. "I've been just horrible. Horrible to Sam. Every little thing – and the big things – he's been doing since I got home from the hospital that day, everything has set me off. I know he just wants to help me, to be there for me, but all the coddling and the 'taking care of me' has just gotten on my nerves so bad. It isn't fair, I know. Not fair of me. Not fair to him. But I can't help the way I feel. I just need him, I need everyone, to stop acting like I'm about to break. Because I'm not." No longer crying, Carrie spoke the last words with conviction. Jude noticed. For the first time, she saw that her friend was not anxious, not even her usual anxiousness. She saw in Carrie's face a newfound strength. "No, no you're not,"

Jude said, "I can see that now. I'm sorry, Carrie, that I didn't see it before. And Sam, well, Sam may take a little longer, but he'll see it too. He was just so scared, so scared at the possibility of losing you." And now Carrie felt the guilt, though she knew Jude hadn't said it for that reason. "I love him. I love him so much," Carrie said. "I just wonder if I even told him this morning as I left that I loved him? Kate," she'd looked at the other woman, "what you said, about taking today off if I needed to, I wonder if you think that would really be possible?" "Sure, honey," Kate answered right away, "I told you everyone would understand." "See, even that would have irritated me earlier, the 'understanding' part," Carrie said. "I just have something I have to do, I have to do it today. It really can't wait."

She arrived back home just before lunch. Sam looked up in surprise and concern when she'd walked into the kitchen through the back door. Before he could even say anything, Carrie held up her hand to stop him. Walking over, she knelt down until she was level with his face from the height of the wheelchair. "Sam, my Sam, I have some things to say, and I want to say them just right. And I need to say them right now. Be patient with me, while I get this all out." Still looking concerned, Sam just nodded. "I need to say some things to you. I love you. You know that. I love you so much. But I don't want or need you to be my protector. I want and need you to be my friend. And so much more. I want and need you to listen to my feelings, about really stupid

103

things and about the more serious things. I want and need you to laugh with me. To hold me just because I'm precious to you and not because you feel like you have to comfort me all the time." When he'd started to speak, Carrie had placed her index finger over his lips, "I'm not finished yet. Just let me finish everything I want to say. I want and need you beside me, every day going forward. Every day of my life. You're the love of my life." She'd reached into her purse, pulled out the tiny jeweler's box then, lifted the lid to show a wide gold band. "Sam, will you marry me?" The words were simple. Words he didn't believe he'd ever hear, not from Carrie. And she was the only one he'd ever wanted to share those words with. She'd made it clear in the past that she didn't want to get married. He had so many questions, but he'd wait until much later to ask those questions. Right now, all he needed to do was give her an answer, as simply as she had asked, Sam said "Yes. Yes let's get married."

Stephen smiled when Emily walked through the front door. Waddling. He always thought she waddled rather than walked, although he didn't dare say that out loud. At eight and a half months pregnant, he thought she was stunning. Even more stunning than that day in her parents' garage when she'd shown so much attitude. Oh, she still had the attitude. If possible, the extra little life inside her doubled it. He often wondered if their child was going to be a handful, knew it likely, all things considered. And couldn't wait for every minute of it. He planned to be right there when their baby came into the world, wanted her, they knew it was a "her," to see his as one of the first faces she ever saw. Wanted to support Emily however her could, even if that meant just taking all the abuse she could hand out while she was in pain. And he never underestimated his wife, so he knew he was in for quite a ride. Greg had told him more than once that he didn't envy him being in that delivery room. Emily had overheard her brother once, a murmured joke to Stephen to the effect that if it walked like a duck and quacked like a duck…and the verbal lashing he took was just an insight into what Stephen would face. The house was nearly done. If such a thing was really possible. They were putting finishing touches in the nursery upstairs, more decoration than renovation though. Even though they were having a girl, Emily didn't want everything to be pink. Instead, she'd decided on natural, neutral colors – beiges and creams. It wasn't traditional for a girl, but since they were so close to the ocean, spent so much time near it and on it, she'd added in a few touches with that in mind. There was a stuffed whale sitting in the new rocking chair in the corner. The one her Dad had bought as soon as he'd heard their news. And the small wall mural on that oddly angled wall was one of rocks and shells on a beach. Stephen had found the seashell windchimes in Maeve's shop himself and picked it up as a perfect mobile for the room. He was going to be the most perfect girl-Daddy, he'd decided. He knew one, just one, reason Emily was so grumpy was because she had her own doubts about being a good mother. But he knew she had been raised by one, and she would be one. No one had a bigger capacity to love than his Emily. They'd thought about names, had gone through the 'Baby Name' books several times. They had three contenders – Sophie Mae, Grace Addison, and Olivia Quinn. But Emily said she wasn't deciding until she met their daughter. She said that *then* they'd know the right name. And it might not even be one of the ones they'd selected. Daily, Stephen would come up with a new, outrageous name he'd toss to Emily over breakfast, just to make her laugh. *Peony Anne. Coral Josephine. Minerva Nicole. Ophelia Marie. Nova Francine. Africa Suzanne. Athena Renee.* Daily they became more outlandish. This morning he'd been especially inspired, he thought, when he'd tossed out *Hominy Jane.* He'd started to worry that Emily might turn the tables on him and actually use one of the names. He could just picture himself calling his daughter down for dinner yelling "Wilhelmina" up the stairs.

Not surprising to Stephen, Emily hadn't slowed down a bit. Despite the waddling. She still went to The Providence Historical Society at least three times a week. Mrs. Nelson had insisted on setting up a small office on the ground level for her, saying that no expectant mother should be climbing all those stairs. Emily didn't agree, argued that the doctor said exercise was good for her and the baby, but Mrs. Nelson and Mrs. Connor had held firm on this decision. And, Emily had to admit that as she got bigger and bigger, she was grateful that the two ladies had won the battle. Oh, they were going to be such wonderful Godmothers. She knew they'd spoil her daughter horribly, but she also hoped that they'd pass along some of their joie de vivre, some of their passion for life to the little girl. She wanted her daughter to be strong and independent and opinionated and not afraid to stand up for her beliefs. If her daughter inherited any of the spunk of Mrs. N and C, she'd be happy. In fact, they were planning a trip, a cruise this time, though it was far enough out that they'd run no risk of missing the birth. She couldn't imagine the two older ladies playing shuffleboard, which was what she imagined first when she thought of a cruise. She'd laughed out loud the day she'd overheard them setting their limits, their *sizable* limits, for gambling on the ship. On the days when she didn't go into the office, Emily could be found working on the book she was developing on the early colonial homes of Providence, from any room in the house. Sometimes Stephen found her in their bedroom, or at the kitchen table, or in his office. Once he had even come upon her in the guest bathroom jotting down notes as she looked out the window with a pair of binoculars. Laughing he'd taken them from her hands, joking "you're going to get arrested for that." Just mentioning the book had given her access to many of the older homes in Providence that she'd always wanted to see. After taking a class at the Bristol Community College in photography, she had happily amassed thousands of photographs. Many, many more than she could possibly use in the book. Stephen had been impressed the first time he'd seen her photos. Not your typical, straight on boring shots of houses. He should have known she wouldn't be typical. At anything. No, the photos she took were often filled with the architectural details of the homes. She would fill a frame with just a carving on a porch corbel, or of the tile surrounding a fireplace. *Somehow,* he thought, *she'd even made the plain, straight moldings and millwork look interesting from that angle.* She used shadows to her advantage. She took photos too of the gardens and the people and the pets in the houses. They were part of the story too, she'd said when he'd asked. Even though she loved the work, her work at the Preservation Society and her work on the book, Emily had to admit that these days her favorite place was on the oversized couch in the living room with Blondie at her feet and Dagwood's head in her lap. *Across* her lap. Her oversized belly had

become the perfect pillow for the two dogs, who seemed
to be on a schedule of taking turns.

Maybe it was time. Both of her girls, that's how she thought of Jude and Carrie, were safe now. Safe and happy. She'd always enjoyed her job, liked seeing the comings and goings. But the last few months had changed things for Kate. Oh, she was still on top of her game. But the recent events had changed her. Changed her priorities. She would always take an interest in BICO, in the people she valued there. But she thought it might be time to do something for herself too. To pay herself back for all the years of work. She deserved some rest, and some adventure, which wasn't very restful but then she thought a lot of rest would be boring. She could certainly afford to do anything she wanted. *So, what did she want to do?* That was the biggest dilemma. She'd worked her entire life, most of it for one organization. So, she'd kept working. Had been there each morning to greet her girls, saw them off at the end of the day. And she went home alone at night. *Was this what growing old was supposed to be?* After several weeks of wallowing in indecision, Kate became fed up with herself. *This was ridiculous. Just pick something, already,* she'd told herself.

At dinner on a Friday evening at Carrie and Sam's house, she'd made her announcement. Jude and Jake had arrived earlier, were comfortably wandering back and forth between the kitchen and the patio. Jake carried a cold brown bottle, Jude had a fruity concoction of some sort with a hot orange umbrella stuck in it. Kate too was sipping something that had come out of the blender, an icy slush that she was certain was more potent than she thought it was. Sam had been playing bartender after all. She'd started to speak, stopped to clear her throat. *Where had that little tickle in the back of her throat come from?* Starting over, she plunged forward. "Today I spoke with Archer." Seeing the blank look on the girls' faces, she'd supplied, "Mr. Henderson." She was the only one who called the Vice President of BICO by his first name. Understanding, but still not knowing where this conversation was headed, the girls nodded as one. "I gave him my notice." There, it was out now. The silence from the girls was complete, though the surprised looks on their faces spoke loudly. They'd known, or guessed, that she was old enough to retire, had made assumptions that perhaps she couldn't afford to retire. Many couldn't. Even more likely, they knew Kate was not the type to just sit home and do nothing. She was a dynamo. They couldn't imagine the company without her. As could none of the other employees since she had been there longer than any of them. Realizing they were being rude, Kate belatedly spoke "Congratulations, Kate. Congratulations. That's great news. We're really incredibly happy for you." Laughing at her, Kate responded, "you're sweet, Jude, but a horrible liar." Patting the younger woman's hand as it lay on the table beside her drink, Kate continued "Oh, I know you mean it. We're family here so there's no need for niceties. You either, Carrie." Carrie walked from the counter to the round table, sat with her two friends. "We are family. That's why we're surprised, Kate. We didn't even know you were thinking about retiring." Smiling because she knew that both girls sincerely meant it when they called her their 'family', Kate knew she had to explain everything. As she took Carrie's hand in her other, "Carrie. My girl. What happened to you a few months ago, well, it happened to me too. To all of us in some way. Oh, I didn't come close to going through what you endured, but the whole thing made me realize how precious life can be. And while I love seeing you both every day, watching the business grow, I had to ask myself if that was where I wanted to stay for the rest of my life. I've been there a very long time, you know. Well, you don't really know, but trust me, it's been a long time. I've thought hard about this, because I just didn't think that I could survive a typical retirement. Sure, it would be nice for a day, but what would I do after that?" Because this had been exactly what Jude had been thinking, she laughed, "You're not exactly the relaxed sort." "Exactly," Kate continued. "That's why I had to think so hard. Not just about leaving BICO but about what I would do after that day. And so, I made some decisions. I'm going to have a second career." Surprised, but not really, Carrie was intrigued. Kate certainly had Jude's interest too, "Do tell," she said. "Well, I do want some rest and relaxation, and I do want to travel. I've never been outside of this state. Not in my whole life. I've never felt the need before to leave it. But now I want to see the world. I want to see palm trees and castles and ancient ruins. I want to see the beauty of the world. I want to smell exotic flowers and taste new foods. I want to explore. To experience. I want to have adventures. I want to ride a camel around The Great Pyramid. To take a slow cruise down the Rhine and sample every wine of that region. To see water that is really that bright crystal blue color you see in photographs online. I want to snorkel in it, or on it, however you do it. Walk through some of those exuberant English gardens. But I know that even if I take some trips, the time in between trips would do me in. I wouldn't be able to just 'hang out' with no responsibilities day-in and day-out. So, I came up with a way to combine both. It took a little marketing on my part, I put together a presentation. I'll admit I used a few contacts to get my foot in the door, just enough to make my pitch. It didn't hurt any that the son of their biggest stockholder had completed a summer internship, years ago, with BICO. He still remembered me, now isn't that wonderful? You, ladies, are looking at the new, and *only*, Director of Seniors Activities for the largest cruise ship line in the world." The grin spread slowly to Jude's face, "Kate, that's perfect! You'll be able to travel, and still have a job, a purpose." "That's right, Jude. I knew you'd see the sensibility of it right off. It wasn't a job that existed, but I did my research. Did you know that the average age of cruise ship passengers inches closer every year to the fifty-year-old mark? Fifty-one percent of all cruise passengers are over the age of fifty. And the industry doesn't even realize that potential. Oh, they take their money, but the opportunities are so much greater. Older passengers would have special needs, and different interests than the younger passengers. I can understand both of those first-hand. I'll be organizing on-board activities as well as overseeing the day trips when we dock in port." Laughing at herself, "Dock in port. Do you hear me? I'm already talking like I know what I'm doing. I'll have the opportunity to vet the expeditions myself personally, see how easily accessible they are, assess any difficulties that an older person might have. So be ready to receive tons of photos in your inboxes. I'll get to plan activities that are more tailored to the older crowd. Still lots of fun, absolutely, just maybe not as strenuous, as physically demanding. I have a rating scale in my head, from easiest to most challenging physically." Carrie looked over at Jude then and said, with a smile, "Of course she does." "And," Kate continued as though there had been no interruption, "if I do say so, events that are more intellectual too. I already have a list of guest speakers and comedians who target an older crowd jotted down. I'll be in charge of the promotions too. Not doing the social media marketing myself but having input and signing off on everything." "Kate that's wonderful," Carrie got up to hug her friend, her mentor, "When do you sail?" "See, now you're catching onto the lingo yourself," Kate laughed. "Actually, I fly on Monday to headquarters in Miami." "Monday! So soon," Jude jumped in. "My, you certainly don't waste any time, do you? You won't even give us time to organize a proper retirement party." "Oh, I don't want one of those."

"Alright then, a Bon Voyage party." "Now that sounds like more fun, but I don't need one of those either. Now, I'm not putting my house on the market, not yet. But if everything works out well, that's for the future. I'll be living on the waves most of the time. Really, all the details have been worked out. Which brings me to one more thing I want to talk to you girls about." Thinking she would ask them to look after the house, which of course they wouldn't mind, Jude was again surprised by what Kate said next. "As of today at noon, I transferred five percent of my BICO stock over to your names. Two and a half percent to each of you. Now, before you say anything," for she'd seen the surprise on Carrie's face, the objection on Jude's, "understand that this isn't all of my stock. Just a part of it. I'll still retain almost twelve percent myself." Smiling smugly at the looks on their faces, she continued, "Yes, I've listened well and invested wisely. What better investment than the company I've poured my heart into for over forty-five years? I bought in right at the beginning, the stocks split several times, I received generous compensation in the form of more stocks from our management a few times. I really don't have to work, but I want to. And there's no way I can spend all my money before I die, especially since my housing and my travel will be mostly paid for by my new employer. I'm set for life. And I know you girls didn't expect it, but I need you to know that I need to do this. For you. As we've already covered, you're my family. And the greatest gift I can give you is freedom, the freedom to do what you want. And I am going to hold you to it. I want you each to take time, figure out what you really want from life. Or at least what you think you want at this stage of your lives. It can change later. I'm proof of that! But I want you to decide, and then I want you to go for it. Whatever it is. Take the money and add your own sweat and brains and create the life you want. I will stipulate that I'd like to see each of you on a cruise, at least once per year." Feeling the need to refuse, but also recognizing the no-nonsense look on Kate's face, the love for them shining in her eyes, Jude realized that to turn down this incredible gift would be stupid. Stupid and hurtful to Kate. She knew the gift had been thought out, not something Kate had taken lightly. Smiling as she held the older woman's fingers in her own, she'd simply said "So, where do we sail to first?"

He'd headed North out of Des Moines, heading towards Minnesota. Hoping the trail, if it was discovered, would lead them to think he was heading for Canada. That's where they'd waste time looking. He figured they could waste a lot of time in Canada. He stopped about 7 miles outside the city limit, grabbed the duffle bag he kept in the back seat always just for this purpose. Positioned and adjusted the expensive toupee until it looked natural. At least it would look natural to any passing motorist who might be paying attention. Put on the thick-framed glasses which had no prescription to the lenses, no, his eyes were perfect. Just like Pop's. He could see everything perfectly. He had no doubt that his description, his name, and his license plate number were being broadcast across the media. He'd used a rest room at one of those travel stop places along the highway, there was only one other car in the parking area. He'd changed his clothes, cleaned himself up, gritting his teeth as he applied antiseptic to the scratches. *That Bitch!* He'd traded the car in Ankeny, just on the outskirts of Des Moines, knowing he was racing a clock and needed to get a different vehicle as quickly as possible. Had switched the license plate with an old spare one he kept in the duffle, again, a part of his contingency plan. So, he was driving a different car, he looked different, and he was headed to Canada. All temporary measures to help him avoid detection. He backtracked into Des Moines then and began heading east. Set the cruise control firmly on 64, not one mile per hour over that, headed for the coast. Glancing at the dashboard, it caught his attention that the light was on for the seat belt. He hadn't buckled himself in after leaving that rest stop. It wasn't like him. He knew experienced State Troopers could spot a driver without a seat belt at a glance. A risk he hadn't meant to take, it had just been accidental. He had other, more permanent means of disguise waiting for him back in Providence. Back home. Simon Krupp no longer existed. His new driver's license, credit cards and other forged identification waited for him there in a small storage locker he had maintained all the while he was in Des Moines. Under his *other* name, the one on the papers there. He had an apartment there too, a three-room downstairs efficiency apartment in the one of the older houses in the quieter end of the Federal Hill neighborhood. It wasn't situated close to any of the trendy restaurants and bars of that area, but it was close to the interstate. He'd kept the rent paid, under his second name, the entire time he had been in Iowa. Because you could just never be too careful, or too prepared, in his mind. If anyone had searched the records, it would appear that he had been living there the entire time he had actually been in Des Moines. It was not a nice apartment, not up to his standards, but that is exactly why it had been chosen. Old linoleum floors in the kitchen and bath that had turned to a dirty tan, even when he scrubbed them to get them as clean as possible. No separate bedroom, he had picked up a pull-out sofa from a resale shop. On the positive side, it was close enough to a grocery store that delivered. All he had to do was pay in advance and give instructions for them to leave the bags on the small porch outside the front door. He never even had to see them. And they never got the chance to see him. He had everything he needed, was self-contained, really no need to go out in public. Except for when he was *working.* He did not look for a new job once he was back in Providence, deciding that it was best to remain out of the public as much as possible. He'd prudently stashed money into several accounts at different banks for years, at least twenty-five percent of each paycheck. And, since he spent so little money, he figured he was good for at least a couple of years before he had to think about an income. For now he would bide his time, work on changing his appearance, do nothing to bring attention to himself. And he would plan, plan what was next. He had to be patient, not move too fast. Be careful.

He was stagnating. He was driving through Providence, but he was stagnating. He knew it but didn't know what do about it. To be fair to himself, his career was fine. He liked the engineering firm and it certainly paid well. Greg Carson was more than comfortable. But that was the problem. Everyone else seemed to be moving straight ahead with life, while he was just staying in one position. Not moving forward. While he liked his job, thought he produced good work, it didn't bring him any satisfaction. His twin had found that. Surprisingly enough, she'd found it as a wife and a soon-to-be-mother. She loved her work and now was swimming in her new book project. She was happy. And he was glad she was happy. Glad too that his best friend was part of what made her happy. His best-friend-turned-brother-in-law. It amazed him sometimes that Stephen had the patience and cunning, because he knew it had taken some, to win Emily over. Someday he'd get the full story out of him. He was starting to think that engineering might not have been the best fit for him. And that thought always brought guilt. He'd think about all the money his parents had paid for his education. Sure, he'd helped out, worked part time during the school year and full time in the summers. But the burden had mostly been theirs. And now, to just throw that away, to admit to them that he'd made a mistake, most of the time he just buried those thoughts and the idea of taking a different road, buried them deep. And speaking of roads, he looked up then, really paid attention, and found that he had ended up on Sanders Street, just a block from Maeve's shop "Irish Blessings." *How had that happened? Well, since he was here anyway…*He liked the sound made by the bells when he opened the door. It wasn't the usual loud clanking he heard in other shops meant to alert the sales staff that someone was either coming or going. No, the sound as he entered this shop was a lighter, tinkling kind of sound. Not surprised at her attention to the detail, he'd glanced up at the multitude of tiny bells strung from vibrant green ribbon. They even *sounded* like her. Everything in the shop spoke of where she had come from, who she was. Most of the merchandise she stocked came directly from the small family businesses in Ireland she favored. There was crystal from Galway displayed beneath the brightest lights to make it sparkle from any spot in the shop. Belleek pottery neatly lined the shelves mounted on the back wall. He noticed a display of perfumes – *were there Irish perfumes?* Maybe he'd buy a bottle for his Mom, earn some brownie points. Her stock certainly was diverse. A beautiful oil painting held his attention for several minutes. Knowing nothing about art, he'd been captured by the simple grassy path that led into the trees. The artist had certainly used every shade of green, just like he'd heard said about Ireland. Another small display counter held silver jewelry. Claddagh rings and what looked like Celtic cloak pens to him. Dangly earrings, the kind Maeve often wore. *And since when did he notice what kind of earrings a woman wore?* There was a small display of palm-sized, smooth rocks painted with spirals and other symbols he was sure were Celtic, although he didn't know what they meant. *Runes, I think they're called. Now I'll have to research that. Maybe a paperweight?* He thought, weighing one in his hand. He wandered past tables of scarves and woven hats and gloves into the apparel room. He saw Aran sweaters, he'd always liked the look, maybe he'd buy one. He'd looked at the price tag and promptly put the cream-colored sweater he'd picked up back with the others. Tried to arrange it, to fold it like it had been, but made a mess of things. He heard laughter behind him as Maeve took the sweater from his hands, managed to fold it neatly so that it made a tidy bundle like all the other sweaters. "Someday, you'll have to show me how you did that," Greg grinned. "Oh, I somehow doubt that's a skill you can master, Greg. To what do I owe this honor? Are you shopping for something, maybe a gift," she hinted. "Sales slow?" he'd asked in commiseration. "It usually is this time of year," she'd answered. "When the weather is nice everyone treks to the beaches and larger cities for vacation. But I do OK. I have some regular customers that I always keep on a list for new items. They want first option when a shipment comes in." "Well then, since you're a little slow today, why don't you let me take you to lunch," he'd suggested smoothly. Well, he thought it was smooth as he'd said it. But he could see from the look on Maeve's face that she wasn't fooled. Nor was she impressed. Grasping for something, he'd rambled on, "actually, you'd be doing me a favor. I need a sounding board." "A what?" she'd asked, tiny furrows forming between her eyebrows. They were cute, he decided, although there wasn't much that was cute about Maeve. Tall and slender, she had the build of a ballerina. There was so much grace in every step she took. *And again, where were these thoughts coming from?* He'd been attracted to her from the beginning, from their first meeting, but it hadn't seemed mutual. And now, she was part of the family, being Emily's friend. He saw her often enough, though usually when they were around other people. "A sounding board," he'd continued, "an impartial listener. Someone I can talk to about something rolling around inside my head. Something I don't want to talk to anyone else about." Intrigued, and recognizing that this wasn't a come-on, Maeve gave him the first genuine, the first personal smile, since he'd entered the shop. "All right. You've made me curious now. Besides, I'm starving! Just let me close up the shop, we won't be gone more than an hour, will we?"

They sat at the tiny iron table on the sidewalk with the matching chairs. Dappled shade danced on the sidewalk as the breeze stirred the leaves overhead. It was nice. Quiet. And he'd always liked the menu here. Yes, it could be a little fancy, he knew, and that might appeal to Maeve. But he had an addiction, a *taste* addiction, to their French Onion Soup and the shredded beef served on the long hoagie with the bowl of dipping broth. He'd placed the order after Maeve had selected the melon and prosciutto salad and bowl of seafood chowder that would come, he knew, with those crackers that looked like tiny pillows. After the waiter filled their water glasses and took their orders, it had been just moments before he'd returned with their drinks. A tall, iced tea with lemon wedges for Maeve and a soda for Greg. "I know," he'd said at the look on her face, "not healthy. Not at all healthy." As he touched his glass to hers, he'd added, "But I live on this. For some it's the caffeine in coffee. Like Emily. You don't want to deprive her of her coffee or she'll turn into a…" searching for the right word, one not too offensive against his sister, he'd paused. Laughing, Maeve had supplied "banshee." He was laughing then too, "Yes, that's the right word. The perfect description. She can turn into a banshee without her coffee. Although she's handled the switch to decaf during the pregnancy pretty well, *for her*, I think. It just amazes me sometimes that my sister is going to be a mother soon. And I'm going to be an Uncle." Maeve's salad and the two soups arrived quickly. Surprising him, she dug right into her food. *Genuine*, he thought. She was always genuine, and that was maybe the thing that drew him to her. Again and again. Glancing up, noticing him staring at her, Maeve had blushed. "Sorry. I told you I was starving. So, tell me what I'm an ironing board for?" "A what? An ironing board?" lost for a moment, Greg had burst out laughing. "No, no, not an ironing board. A sounding board." "I knew it was wrong when I said it," she laughed at herself, "that's just not a phrase we use in Ireland. Sorry, go ahead and talk to me." He hadn't thought he wanted to talk about it, about the feelings that had been steadily growing inside him. But found, once he started that he couldn't stop. He couldn't, didn't edit anything he said. He told her everything. About his current job. About how he felt like he was stuck, like his life wasn't going anywhere. She'd listened carefully. Really listened to every word. Paid attention to the expressions that moved across his face. Picked up on the emotions in his voice. By the time he finished talking, their plates were empty and being removed by their waiter, who's asked "Dessert? Today we offer fresh apple pie served a la mode and with a wedge of cheddar as an option. Of if you prefer cake, there is the lemon crumb cake with raspberry drizzle." Maeve had surprised Greg when she'd promptly jumped on the apple pie and a cup of coffee. Before this lunch, he wouldn't have thought she ate much more than a child, she was so thin. *Misconceptions.* He adjusted his impressions and found he liked this Maeve better. Better than the Maeve he had created in his head.

Amanda Adams was happy with her life. She'd accomplished much, she thought, in her short thirty-one years. She'd moved from the morning anchor spot into the lead anchor on the evening news just three years after joining the news station. The power anchor. She was fed the best news stories, didn't have to deal with any of the fluff interest stories generated to create human interest or fill time. Six months earlier she had succeeded, after a great deal of pushing, in taking the first step into the News Direction position. Her career was right on target. She had plans to move, eventually, beyond the station, the largest in Providence, to an even bigger one in Boston or Philadelphia. In her business, you had to keep moving in order to move up. As for her personal life, she was winning there too. She'd caught the eye of the Head of Surgery for the Hasbro Children's Hospital. It hadn't taken them long to decide they made a good power couple. She knew that when the time came, he too would be willing to move on to bigger and better things. Their large brick mansion covered in ivy in the Blackstone neighborhood was perfect for their social standing in the city. It wasn't a gated community, for its roots went back much farther than that practice common today. It was established, and stately, and discreet in that way that spoke of money. Lots of money. He'd watched her for weeks. She had no routine, other than that she spent most of her time at work. *Not a good wife at all.* The house was a no-go, he'd known that right away. She was seldom there alone. Cleaning staff, gardeners, and a cook were there all day, even if she wasn't. Her husband's routine was as sporadic as hers, so it couldn't be predicted which nights he would be home and which he wouldn't. And he knew there was security, alarms set that would sound if he even went near the house. And security cameras to capture his every move. No, it couldn't be at the house. And the news station wasn't a good option either, too much coming and going, too many people there. Too much activity. He could do this, he knew he could. He had to do this. Because she deserved it. Because he needed to get even with the whore. And because he needed to prove to himself that he still had what it took. He was taking no chances this time, not after that mistake in Des Moines. He'd retrieved the gun and bullets he had hidden in the storage locker along with his new ID. It was the surest way. Just do it quickly and get out of there. He had learned his lesson. He just had to find a way, a place, a time.

Nothing presented itself, no opportunity. He'd decided he had to make his own opportunity. It would be tricky, he knew. He had to do it so that he didn't get caught. He'd use her ambition against her, would lay a trap. He'd giggled at that thought, remembering the traps he'd set in the woods as a teenager. He'd come so far since then. He'd have to take a few risks, like making the phone call himself, but they couldn't be avoided. He'd called the station on a Wednesday morning, knowing she didn't have to be on the air until later that evening. She was working, he'd made sure her car was there, but not work that she couldn't leave if she needed to. He just had to dangle the right bait. Calling the station was a calculated risk. He knew that someone would be answering the phone and would likely remember it *afterwards,* possibly even enter it into a log. So he had to be careful. He had to convince the person answering the phone that he had to speak with Amanda Adams directly. Had to grab Amanda's attention with an unbelievable opportunity. *Unbelievable,* he'd giggled because it wouldn't be true, but she wouldn't know that. He'd made the call at 10:40 am using a burner cell phone, which he would dispose of later. Had, in a normal voice, introduced himself to the man who answered the phone as Peter Brown, a perfectly plausible, generic name. And not his own. Nor was it the one he was using now. At first, the secretary fielding the calls had not wanted to connect him through to Amanda. She was very busy and yada yada yada. He would take down his number and note the reason for the call and she could return the call at her convenience. Simon knew a brush off when he heard one. He'd bet that Amanda didn't return even one out of every fifty calls that came through for her. He'd turned it up a notch "Look, this wasn't my idea. It was *hers.* She gave me this business card and told me to call her if I ever changed my mind and was willing to tell what I know. *Confidentially. Off the record,* If she's not interested, I'll just go to someone else. I don't need this hassle." He'd been put on hold, listening to the muzak play in the background. When the receptionist called Amanda's desk and relayed the caller's comments, Amanda didn't recall recently giving her card to anyone and asking him to contact her about a big story, but it was something she had done in the past. Who knew how long ago or how big of a story this man might break? Even older, cold stories could be big news with new details. Her pulse began to race after speaking with the man just a few minutes. He spoke in a slightly hushed voice, like he didn't want anyone to overhear, as he tempted her with details about a political scandal that would rock the state, possibly the whole east coast. Just enough details. Dropped just the right names into the mix. A scandal involving money and sex and drugs. Excited, she hadn't thought twice when he told her he wanted to meet privately away from the station. He did not want his name brought into the story in *any* way. *Ever.* He'd stressed just the right words. Assuring him she understood, they'd made plans to meet right after lunch, at a place of his choosing. "Someplace with no one around to see me talking to you," he'd said, "you're recognizable and if anyone connects me to you after the story breaks, I'll lose my job for sure. And that might not even be the worst thing they'd do to me." Her ambition had her agreeing, not even considering whether it would be safe.

When she didn't return to the station for her appearance on the evening news, everyone knew something was wrong. She might not be well liked at the station, but she would never miss an opportunity for airtime. For publicity. Her own publicity. Of course, the anchor of the noon news had jumped at the chance to fill her shoes, just temporarily of course. *That was unless he could make it a permanent filling of said shoes.* When Amanda Adams hadn't returned home for dinner as expected, everyone knew something was wrong. They were having guests for dinner, another power couple that combined the entertainment industry and an esteemed old family name recognizable throughout the east coast. Throughout the whole country, actually. No, Amanda wouldn't miss this dinner for any reason, her husband recognized that even as he fumed that she wasn't there. Making the excuse, which really wasn't an excuse, that he needed to contact the local authorities to report his wife missing, he had gained a few points as the concerned, caring husband and gained some sympathy he could use at a later date, if need be. The anchor who had stepped in to take Amanda's place on the news was the one who had to, *got to*, break the story to the public about the missing newswoman the next day. Employing every acting skill he possessed, he'd appeared sincerely concerned about his missing co-worker and pleaded for any information about her location to be shared with the authorities *as soon as possible.* Several days passed, and the story grew. Search teams were organized for areas around the station and the Blackstone neighborhood. Volunteers and professionals walked in straight lines to cover the open field of grass behind the home. Scent hounds were brought in. He watched the news reports, laughed out loud when he'd heard the reporter, the *male* reporter who had taken her spot, lament about his missing co-worker. *Yeah, I bet you're real sorry. Real worried.* A smile, a genuine smile, though if there had been anyone there to see they would have noted the erratic glaze to his eyes as he smiled, had spread across his face when he'd seen the news conference several days later of the distressed husband. He knew the man wasn't sincere. Hell, while he'd been watching he'd noted that the husband and wife didn't spend any more than four or five waking hours each week together. They were too *career oriented.* Which was fine for the man, to a certain degree, although he should have been home every evening instead of working late. Like Pops had always made it a point to come straight home after work. And as for Amanda, well, she should have produced at least a few children by her age and should have given up her career to raise them. It was an opportunity lost, he felt, considering that these two had enough money to build a strong family together. But they'd let other things take priority. *So, they deserved what they got.* "One down," he'd said the words out loud in his tiny kitchen.

The following week Maeve looked up from the front counter as the shop door opened. "My," she was surprised, "twice in as many weeks. I wasn't expecting this. Am I to be a sounding board again?" Smiling because she'd gotten the phrase correct this time, Greg answered "No, not exactly. I don't need an ironing board today," which brought a laugh from Maeve. "No, but I am here to ask another favor." Pretending disappointment, Maeve joked "well, I guess that's another sale lost then." Greg reached down to the end of the counter, picked up a chunky coffee mug that read "Kiss Me, I'm Irish," sat it in front of her and said "There. There's your sale. Now, do you think that would buy me a little of your time this coming Sunday? If you don't already have plans." "Well," hesitating slightly, she'd asked, "What did you have in mind?" "You're always careful, aren't you?" he'd asked, sincerely interested to know if she was always that way or just with him. "So, as a favor – and you can always say 'No' to favors – would you come with me on Sunday to my parents' house for dinner. It's family dinner night," he rushed on when he saw she meant to say 'No.' "It's family dinner night and I've decided I want to tell them – the whole family – what I've been thinking. Thinking and feeling. Emily and Stephen will be there too. It's not formal, we just get together every week. Makes Mom happy." "Ah," Maeve softened her expression, because she could see that it made him happy too, "so then am I to be a buffer or am I there as a support?" "Maybe both," Greg admitted. "Do you mind?"

He'd picked her up at eleven thirty, his Mom always served promptly at one o'clock. He'd insisted on picking her up rather than meeting her there, "I owe you," he'd said, "this is a favor, remember?" Hardly a favor when she saw the table set with scrumptious foods. It looked like a banquet. Taking her seat, Maeve saw mashed potatoes and baked cauliflower with parmesan breadcrumb topping, and a massive pan of meatloaf that made her eyes widen. "Mom's famous meatloaf," Emily commented, "you're in for a treat. That is, if I leave any of it for anyone else." Laughing, Maeve had to admit that her friend was definitely bigger even than the last time she had seen her a few weeks earlier. Stephen hadn't commented, prudently, had just reach across and patted her belly. *They are so good together,* Maeve thought. Stealing a glance at Greg, she saw much that same thought mirrored on his face. That and such undiluted love when he looked at his sister that it nearly took her breath away. *He gives his whole heart,* she thought and was shaken by that thought. That was just what she had always wanted. No half-way or partial love, she wanted the all-the-way kind of love that lasted forever. She prided herself that she kept her romantic nature a secret. Maybe she needed to loosen up, just a little, where Greg was concerned. They'd all laughed uproariously when Greg's Mom came from the kitchen wearing potholders and sat an individual, though not small, pan of meatloaf in front of Emily. "All yours, baby girl," she'd said. "My baby girl who is going to have her own baby girl." "Mom," Emily pleaded, "Don't go getting misty-eyed. You know the hormones will have me joining you and we'll both end up crying. And the men will all stand around not knowing what to do about it. Besides, your granddaughter is particularly hungry today, she's been punching me for about the last hour, wanting fed." It was an easy meal, comfortable and relaxed, just like Maeve thought a family dinner should be. The perfect balance mixed with some family humor as they'd poked fun at each other, but gently. After they'd finished eating, before the dishes could be cleared, Greg had cleared the lump in his throat, decided it was time to jump in. "Mom, can that wait? Please. Just for a little while. There's something I'd like to talk to you about. Something I need to tell you. All of you," he'd said as he looked around the table at their faces. "Well, all of you except Maeve. She already knows." Maeve saw the look of speculation that came to his mother's face and found herself blushing. Again. Greg had brought more blushes out of her than she could remember as a teenager when living just outside Dublin. "So," Greg started, hesitated and then started again. "Well, you see..." And again, "It's like this..." "Oh for heaven's sake Greggie," Emily said with no small amount of exasperation, "just spit it out already. Whatever it is? You've got us all waiting now." Frowning only slightly at his sister, Greg continued, "OK. OK, As Emily pointed out, this isn't easy for me. To say these things." "Son, is something wrong?" Greg's father asked from the end of the table, concerned now. "No, no, Dad. Nothing is wrong. Well, not like that. I'm fine. Healthy. Not in any trouble." He'd taken a couple of breaths, was surprised when he heard Maeve's voice, "quit stalling Greg. Just tell them." Turning to her, she'd said more quietly, "It'll be alright. I promise." He'd lost himself for a moment in her eyes, just long enough to overcome the case of jitters he had developed. "OK. Here goes. First, I want to say how much I appreciated you, Mom and Dad, paying for my degree at MIT. I know it wasn't easy. Especially with Em and I both in school at the same time. And I know a lot of students didn't have that luxury. And I want you to know that I intend to pay you back every penny." "Now Greg, you know we don't..." This had come from his father, but Greg interrupted, "I mean it, Dad. I am going to pay you back the entire amount. I want to. I need to. And when I say what I am about to say next, you'll understand why." Glancing at Maeve for encouragement, he turned back to his family, "I'm going back to school. For another degree. A Teaching degree." *There, he'd said it. Got it all out. There was no taking it back now.* He'd looked at the faces he knew, the ones he loved, searched for their honest reactions. Had choked on a laugh when his Dad said, "Oh. Well. OK. That's nice son. Now, Gail, can we bring out that big chocolate cake that I might have accidentally stuck my finger into earlier?" "Dad," Greg said, "Did you understand me? I just said that I'm throwing away the engineering degree you paid for, giving up a good job, and am going back to school to become a teacher." Smiling, his Mom reached across the table and placed her hand on her son's. "He heard you, Greg. We all did. Really. Although that's not what we heard. We heard you say that you wanted more, more than you have right now. That you want to be happy. And that what will make you happy is to be a teacher. And you're going to take the steps to get there." Looking back at Maeve, at a loss of what to say, he'd heard her say "it's OK, Greg. It's all going to be OK. In fact, it's going to be great. You can't fail. Not with this family behind you." He'd reached down, covered her hand where it rested on his arm with his own, gave a squeeze.

Art heard the news report. The name – Amanda Adams – clicked in his brain immediately. *The reporter.* The one who had read their prepared statement. She was missing. Never one to assume anything was a coincidence, he had immediately been suspicious. *After all this time had passed, had the killer emerged again?* He considered, for just a moment, not sharing his suspicion with the group. But found himself, late that Thursday afternoon, telling them about the connection of the missing woman to their case. Most had heard the missing persons report, heard the media reports. When he heard of the connection, Les had immediately commented "That's no coincidence. You don't think it is either, do you?" Directed at Art, the former policeman had shaken his head negatively, "No. No, I don't think it is. I do not understand why the killer has been silent for so long, we all know serial killers in general do not stop killing. He may have been incarcerated for another crime. Or, if he has been active, it has all been under the radar. My Captain from the force, he was my Captain when we were investigating, called me last night to let me know about the relationship between the missing woman and our case. He knew, of course, that I would have picked up on it immediately, and he didn't have to call me, he did it just out of mutual respect. And I really appreciate it. I think he knows how much that case took out of me, towards the end of my career. Anyway," he'd cleared his throat, getting back into the business at hand rather than a personal conversation, "one possibility I think we should look into is that our killer was active, but elsewhere." They all noted that he had stopped saying "I" so much over the past months and most often spoke of "Us." He'd become part of the group, had accepted them and they him. They were a unit now, maybe not an official one, but they were a team. And every team member had his or her strengths. "Ann," Art continued, turning to the woman sitting at the end of the table, "I know that you worked for many years as an archivist at the Providence Public Library. Do you still have access to records, or the ability to search records nationwide? I know it's asking a lot, and I am not asking you to break any laws or go against ethics. Keep everything above board. Is it possible?" Leaning in, Ann answered "the library is for public use. Anyone can use any of the resources there for whatever reason. There are no laws or ethics to be concerned about. The average visitor wouldn't necessarily know all the complexities of the key words or search engines, but I think I can manage. Tell me what information you want me to look for, the more detailed the better. In today's age, there aren't many secrets from the internet. The trick is knowing what's real and what isn't, knowing how to find what you're looking for." In a brainstorming session, following Art's lead, the group had compiled a careful list of phrases for Ann. "What makes it so difficult was the randomness of the killings. There was almost nothing in common," Art commented, "other than that the victims were all women." Thoughtfully, Ann agreed, "Yes, that will make searching much more difficult. A search for all unsolved murder cases or missing persons cases where the victim is a woman is going to yield a massive number of results, I'm afraid." Her brother Jim then suggested "I know our killer may have been active before the known Providence cases, but we know the date of the last known murder here and the date Amanda Adams went missing. Can you use those dates to bracket the search results, maybe make the list smaller?" "That's a good idea, Jim" Les agreed, "and geographically limit the searches to the US, I think." "That's good," Ann commented, "keep thinking along those lines. Anything we can come up with the narrow the search would be helpful. I'll get started tomorrow and have at least a partial list by the next time we meet. It may be a long list, though, I'm warning you." "Maybe not as long as you think," Art commented, "I have more faith in the American police force, in their ability to solve crimes, than that. I think if you can narrow the search to cases that have remained unsolved for, let's say three months or more, that would be good too. It would eliminate brand new cases, likely to be solved soon. If there's one thing we know, it's that our killer is careful, and he doesn't get caught." "At least not *so far*," Kathy had commented.

And now the clock was ticking for him, only it was a race and no longer a case of waiting. He'd known, had prepared, that as soon as the whore was reported missing, he would have to keep moving forward. Quickly. There was one other whore who had her dues coming, one more job he needed to do before he could move on. He didn't think of it as escaping, because in his mind he still had done nothing wrong. He had everything lined up for when that time came. His passport, under his new name, with a new photograph. He looked quite different in it, he mused, although he desperately wanted to shave the hair off his head. It was starting to grow out now. He'd put on 34 pounds, filling out his once-thin frame. More than anything, he'd been pleased that this had changed the shape of his face. In addition to increasing his food intake, he'd daily mixed at least two weight-gain shakes. It hadn't been hard to put the weight on, and he was certain that once he was settled in Montenegro, he could take it off just as quickly. He'd despised the changes, knew it make him look lazy and fat, but it was necessary. Yes, once he was finally settled, he would be able to take off the weight, at least some of it. It might be a good idea to keep about half, just so he could appear different from his time spent in the US. He would have his hair cut, though not shaved, as it grew out, might possibly consider dying it dark brown. He'd blend in better, he thought, in his new home with dark brown hair. He'd chosen Montenegro as his ultimate home because, among other things, it had no extradition treaty with the US. It was small, situated on the still-backward Balkan peninsula that just hadn't caught up with the rest of the world. The cost of living was cheap, he had looked into it. It was estimated that he could live there for as little as seven hundred US dollars a month, though he estimated it lower because he planned to be very frugal. He had money stashed in a bank there, and more in nearby Croatia. He'd always been good with money, still had profit made from the money that came out of Mom and Pop's insurance policies. He'd learned too that a fair number of locals spoke English. That would come in handy, when he needed it, but still give him some anonymity too since he could always use the language barrier to his advantage. He would learn the language once he was settled, it was always good to know what was being said at all times. He'd read that the country was still struggling with communications because several regional languages were still popular. He could live there, comfortably he thought, and safely, for the rest of his life. He'd always liked the mountains. He might even get married there, have a few kids. Start a new life. After his responsibilities here were met.

This one would be easy, he'd thought. He knew where she lived. Had known, even before he left Providence before. The big old house. He still liked the idea of burning down the house, with her in it, but after the last few baubles, he was less likely to take risks now. He wanted only guaranteed results. No, a gun was definitely the better way to go. It had worked well with Amanda. The news reports were starting to die down, searches had turned up nothing. Some were speculating that she had just left, left her husband and her life there. No report or news article had mentioned the phone call, the call from the unknown man who had called the station on morning of her disappearance. But he had no doubt that the cops had made note of it. It was just the sort of thing they would hold close, keep quiet. *They'll never find her* he told himself, not this one, he had learned his lessons. He'd made sure of it this time.

He'd driven by the house twice since coming home. Hadn't seen the whore, or the lawyer either, but he knew they were there because the dogs were outside and there were three vehicles parked in the driveway. He planned to catch her when she was leaving one day, that would allow more time before it was noticed she was missing. He just needed a little more surveillance. And a way to get some inside information, about her, about her life.

Stephen saw the car slow near the end of the drive, noticed the man driving the car rolling the passenger's window down and leaning over to speak to him. "Excuse me, can you help me out please?" He'd walked over, had listened as the man explained. "We're moving here, my wife and me. I noticed that attorney sign there, by the side door. Is that by any chance you?" Openly, Stephen had answered "Yes, yes, I am an attorney. How can I help you?" "So, like I said, my wife and I are moving here to the Providence area. We need to sell our house in Indianapolis before we can buy a house here. We haven't had any takers. We've talked about selling it under contract but really don't know how that works. We'd need a lawyer, right? Is that the kind of thing you could handle for us?" It felt rusty, like a skill he hadn't used in a long time, talking to this man. Having a conversation. Even if it was all a lie. "Yes, yes, I could handle that. If you would like to make an appointment," Stephen had offered as he'd passed his business card through to window, "just call this number. It's my law firm downtown office, not here at the house. A secretary there will answer and get your information, schedule an appointment for you and your wife." "Boy, I really appreciate this," the man was grinning. *Boy, do I ever.* "This is great. So tell me, is this an OK neighborhood? A good place for us to look for a house?" "Yes, though most of Providence is safe, my wife and I like living here. It's one of the older neighborhoods, quiet with good neighbors. If you'd like, I'll get contact information for local realtors and have it available for you when we meet." Distracted now, the man had mumbled something that sounded like *wife,* but Stephen hadn't caught the comment. "That would be nice of you," he'd said as he'd driven off. *Strange guy* Stephen had thought. It was like he'd changed his mind there at the end, Stephen wouldn't be at all surprised if no appointment was made. Just a feeling he had, an impression. But there were strange people in the world.

My wife and I like living here, that's what he'd said. *His wife. Would it be the same one, or a different woman,* he'd wondered as he'd driven down to the parking lot of the giant superstore, where he parked his car. Giving the Lawyer time to get a safe distance away from the house. He had to know. After forty minutes, he'd backtracked. Had parked his car on the other side of the street and down about a block and a half. After an hour and a half he'd thought *I don't know how cops do this. How they stand it. Surveillance. It's so boring.* He didn't remember it being this boring before. *She's wasting my time.* Just as the thought ended, he'd seen the front door open, saw the two dogs rush outside, run straight to the bushes in the front yard. Paying attention now, he'd witnessed the woman, the *same* woman, walk to the edge of the porch, laughing at the dogs. *She's pregnant.* That was the only thought that could penetrate the haze. *She's pregnant now. And married.* This changed things. He still had enough control to realize that this changed things. She was no longer in the category. No longer an option. Maybe this was better, he'd thought. Better to just move on now. He already knew that there were direct flights from T.F. Green International Airport to Podgorica. He'd checked that detail months ago to build it into his plan after he'd decided on a destination. Maybe he'd go ahead and book a flight now, maybe go next week. Two weeks might be better, give him enough time to move more accounts around, remotely set up appointments for housing options there.

As they'd waited at the table in the room they'd reserved at the community center, Ann had approached and set a dark blue binder in front of each of them. Jim had teased "she's compulsively organized. Can't help it." To which Ann had stuck her tongue out at him, reminding Art that these two were still brother and sister, even into their later years. "Nice job, Ann," Art commented as he flipped through the pages. "I think I needed you back when I had to prepare all those police reports. That was the worst part of the job, you know?" Happy that he approved of the work she had done, Ann took the lead to explain what they were all looking at. "OK. So I did like we talked. I ran research functions using key words, a time frame, filtered out really recent murders. And, like I thought, that still yielded an enormous number. Over three hundred, actually." "Three hundred," Les was shocked, "we'll never be able to sort through three hundred murders." "Well," said Ann, "I did warn you." Then looking at Art, she continued, "I hope you don't mind, but I took it a step further and did a little more digging. Just in case you thought it had some value, and we can disregard this just as easily as we can add it into the mix, on this second list here, starting on page 4, prioritized them based on location. Proximity to Providence. I thought it might have some value to start with the closest first, since we knew for a fact that our serial killer was active here in Providence. I also ran a cross-refence program," she continued, "to highlight only those locations with multiple unsolved cases." Impressed, Art and the rest of the group spent the better part of an hour looking at the lists. Every name on the lists wasn't just a number, not to Art, it was another victim, a victim whose family still waited for closure. It was overwhelming. Although he kept it to himself, he decided right then that he would devote time on a regular basis during his retirement to look into these unsolved cases. He might not be able to solve them all, or even any of them he admitted humbly, but he sure could try. He had a new direction. And he knew the perfect group of people to help him out.

Refocusing onto the pages, knowing that Ann would be able to answer his questions faster than he'd be able to study all the documents, he'd asked, "Any cities in particular stand out during your research, Ann? Particularly mid-sized cities like Providence?" Smiling, she'd answered, "Yes. There were concentrations of unsolved murders against women in Denver, Colorado and Des Moines, Iowa and Portland, Oregon and Ukiah, California. At least three in each of those cities, all within the right time frame. And in New York City, of course, but that isn't a medium-sized city if you want that filter." Thinking out loud, Al commented, "Seems to me all of those locations are west of here. Not that you can go much east of Providence." He'd stepped to the maps he always carried to the meetings, drawn a circle around the cities. After studying the maps a little longer, he'd wondered "in order to get to any of these cities, our killer would probably have left Providence on I-95. Then, since they're all in the northern half of the US, he'd probably have taken I-80." He'd marked the roads on the map with a yellow highlighter. "That's good, Al," Art commented. "We're starting to get a picture here. At least it's something to think about." Ann had been flipping through her research, "Just as a mention, there was one unsolved murder of a woman in Pennsylvania along that route that meets our criteria. Her name was Marilyn Harris, she was a waitress at a truck stop. Went home after work one day and didn't report back the next. They found her in her apartment, she'd been strangled with a cord." Stopping, because it hit her then that they were talking about a real person, she'd sat, looked at Art for several minutes. "How did you stand it?" she'd asked. He'd understood the question. "It is hard. It's really hard. You see some terrible things happen to people who just don't deserve them. And you can't save them all. You just have to remember the ones you do save. Whether it's a domestic violence situation or a school shooting or kids on drugs, there are always some you save. That has to get you by. You don't forget the ones you can't save. Couldn't even if you tried." After a few moments while they all thought about what he'd said, Todd picked up the trail where they'd left off. "So if we place him near that truck stop, that apartment in Stroudsburg, it only seems logical that he would have continued along the same road. Right?" Ann had recovered from the emotions brought on by her realizations and jumped back into the conversation.

"There was another murder, just a single murder, after the one in Stroudsburg, that follows the roads Al marked on the map. It was in Starved Rock State Park in Illinois. A young woman, in her twenties. She'd stayed behind while her group of friends went hiking because of an injury. After the others came back to the cabin, they found her there. She'd been shot. Her name was Shelley." "And if we connect those locations," Jim commented, "the next city of the size we're targeting on that route would be Des Moines, Iowa. And it's on Ann's list." Knowing that they easily could be off track, be looking in the wrong area and at the wrong murders, Art couldn't help but feel like they were accomplishing something. Not wanting to stop, to put it off for another week, he'd suggested, "are any of you interested in staying later tonight to continue? We could order pizza delivery. I'd like to go over the details of the Des Moines cases before we end it for the week. If any of you don't want to stay, it's fine, really." Of course they'd all stayed. As they were breaking up later that night, Art told the group, "I know an agent. An FBI Agent who worked with us on the Providence cases. I'm going to call him tomorrow, share our thoughts with him. See if he knows anything, or can find out anything, about the cases in Des Moines, Anything that might not be widely circulated information."

Had there been more information? Oh, yes, there had been. Although Art hadn't expected it, Agent Alexander had shared with him information which had not been widely circulated. *A name.* They knew the name of a man in Des Moines who had kidnapped a woman and would likely have killed her. He'd also made reference, during that event, to others, leading the woman to believe he had killed women in the past. "His name was Simon Krupp. But he's gone under the radar. Local agents interviewed his sister living there. As is common, she was shocked and adamant that this could not be her brother. He was a wonderful brother and uncle, she'd said, a perfect son too. We ran some background on the guy. He fit the profile fairly well. Didn't tick every box, but enough of them. The problem is they can't find him. I looked deeper after your call earlier today, into his background. Get this, he originally came from Providence. According to his employer, one of those big insurance firms, he started working there just three months after the last murder in Providence. Another interesting thing from his file – apparently his father killed his mother when our guy was just in college. Dad went to prison, but got taken out by a fellow inmate not long in. Together, that makes a pretty disturbing picture. We really need to find this guy. We need to talk to him, ask some questions. You think he's back in Providence now?" "I do," said Art. "In some way, some crazy way, it all makes sense. The recent disappearance of Amanda Adams, the reporter we fed that story to. It has to be a connection. But this guy, he's smart. Really smart. He hasn't gotten by with this for so long without being smart. Can we get a photo from Des Moines, circulate it in the Providence media? Surely, they have one, right, since they had the name? He probably doesn't use that name, not now, he's too smart for that, but a photo could blow things wide open."

Just as Emily rounded the newel post, rubbing the round knob on top that she herself had once sanded and stained, lovingly, her water broke. Shocked, she felt the release of the pressure, the wetness down her legs. She'd been in shock, disbelief. *Was this really happening?* Oh, she'd known for the past seven and a half months that she was pregnant after first using the little stick-test she'd bought at the pharmacy. She'd taken it all in stride, she thought. She hadn't whined, not overly, as she'd grown to the size of beach ball. She had bitched a little about the stretch marks but had loved Stephen even more when he dropped the little bag on her lap one night. Peaking inside she'd discovered a tube of belly cream. Tempted, for just one moment, to tease Stephen that he had done it just because he didn't want to always have to look at the marks into the future, she'd instead just walked to him, hugged him to her. He knew her so well. But she really would have liked to have been a mouse in the store when he'd tried to explain what he wanted. Oh, that must have been hysterical. Maybe she'd get him to tell her the details someday. Not laughing now, she'd called out for him, her voice growing hysterically. Stephen heard her through his closed office door. Unbelievably, she sounded, well, not like herself at all. She sounded scared. And that scared him. He ran to her, but she held up her hands for him to stop. "Wait, stop.

Be careful you don't fall." Not understanding, he'd looked at the floor, had seen the puddle beginning to spread from…from Emily. Without saying a word, he'd reached for her, picked her up, walked through the living room into the kitchen and out the back door. The bag was already in the car. Tucking her inside, he'd glanced at her face for a moment, she was being uncommonly quiet. For his Emily. He saw such love there, shining for him, that it almost took his breath. He just had to hold it together now, to get them safely to the hospital. He'd pushed the Bluetooth button as he drove, made the call to their pediatrician, told him that they were on their way to the hospital. The second call was answered quickly. "Mom, Mom it's happening. We're on our way now, can you meet us there?" Though tearful, Gail had been laughing with joy, "Yes, we're right behind you. And I'll call Greg for you. You just get our girl there all in one piece."

Somehow, he did get her there. Got them both there. Knew in the instant he helped her through the doors, that his part had just begun. He stayed by her side, through every pain and every breath. As Greg had predicted, Emily let loose with a string or cusswords that had the nurses embarrassed, even the experienced ones who'd heard it all before. He was so proud of her. His had been the first face his daughter saw as she came into the world. Screaming the whole time, a fact that wasn't lost on him. She was going to be just like her mother. And nothing could have pleased him more.

After the nurses had cleaned her daughter, and Emily too, as the pain killers began to take effect, she had looked into her tiny daughter's face and felt so much love. More than she'd expected. Had never even imagined that it was possible just to *feel* so much. Smiling through the tears at her husband, her rock, she'd said, "Look. Look, Stephen. Isn't she perfect?" and, just as her parents came through the door, "Stephen, I don't think you've been properly introduced. To your daughter. Meet Stephanie Rose." And that was the moment that Stephen broke down, overcome with emotions, "You're naming her Stephanie? For me? Are you sure?" "Oh yes, yes, I'm very sure. I always want her to have your strength, your capacity for understanding and forgiveness. I may have some strength of my own, but the other traits are all yours and she'll need them."

She'd hurried. Closed the shop and rushed as fast as she could. These things were supposed to take some time, right? Especially with the first one. She hadn't made it. She'd taken time to run into the gift shop. Mindful of Emily's nursery decor, she'd finally found just the right thing. A pretty replica of the Point Judith Lighthouse, the real thing was just down the coast. And then she'd seen the cute little stuffed lobster and had to get it too. Oh, and those pretty pink tulips in the floral refrigerator for Mommy. Mommy deserved a present too. Rushing with her arms full of flowers, holding the gift bags by the cords, Maeve had nearly run over Emily's Mom in the hallway. "Oh, Hi! Is she here yet? I'm not too late, am I?" Laughing, Gail had never Maeve so disheveled. Granted, she didn't know her all that well, had met her through Emily. She'd talked to her at some of the parties Emily and Stephen had thrown. Always found her to be a level-headed girl. And that beautiful lilting Irish accent, that was a charm. Considering, though, the interaction she had seen between Maeve and her son, she'd been working her way up to some alone time with the younger woman. Get to know her a little better. Not that she didn't trust either her son's or her daughter's choices in partner. Look how splendid Emily had done. Stephen was the best son-in-law that a mother could ask for. And now, now, they had gifted her with the most perfectly perfect grandbaby ever. "Slow down, Honey," Gail had laughed at Maeve. "It's true though that you have missed the main event. Once she made up her mind, my granddaughter wasted no time. She wanted to rush out into the world. I think this should give us some inkling of what her personality is going to be like." Seeing Maeve's disappointed face, Gail had continued, "Emily is resting right now, why don't you give me *these*," she'd taken the massive bouquet from Maeve's arms, "aren't they just gorgeous? I'll take them in and arrange them into a vase, so they'll be the first thing Emily sees when she wakes up. Stephen's going to be in trouble if you bring flowers and he doesn't. I think I should gently nudge him in that direction. He's so proud, Maeve, beaming from ear to ear. Oh, and you brought other presents too." "For the baby," Maeve answered, "I remembered the beach theme of the nursery and just couldn't resist." Peaking inside, Gail smiled at the lighthouse, "Well, the lighthouse is symbolic, you know. A guiding light. So I think that's about perfect. And well, this guy here," she said as she pulled the lobster from the bag, "he's certainly something isn't he?" Not sure if that was as compliment or not, Maeve had laughed. *Oh me, she even laughs in Irish,* Gail had thought. It was certainly easy to see why Greg was attracted to this woman. Though she was more serious, more contemplative, than any other woman he had ever dated. She paid attention to details, Gail made that judgement based on the thought that had gone into the gifts. "Why don't you do on down to the nursery floor and take a peek at our beauty. Don't lose your heart now, I know I did. Emily may be awake by the time you come back." She knew, of course, that Greg was there, she'd left him just a few minutes earlier making silly faces at Stephanie. *That ought to do it,* she'd thought. *No way could Maeve resist that.*

Maeve stepped off the elevator into the sterile hallway. Looking right and then back left, she'd spotted Greg standing at the large window. He wasn't moving, she noticed. Just standing so still. As she'd approached, he looked up into her eyes. His were overflowing. Surprised, *how did he always surprise her?* Maeve moved so that she was standing beside him. "Which one?" she'd asked, then looked where he pointed. Maeve laughed at the tiny bundle who was doing everything possible to become unbundled. "She doesn't like being wrapped up, does she?" Still crying, and laughing too, Greg smiled at Maeve. Later, she would remember *that was what did it. The tears and the laughter, how he couldn't hold either one inside.* Putting her arm around him, they'd stood together, watching the battle that waged behind the glass between the nursery assistant and the swaddled baby. "Oh, she's going to be so much fun, isn't she?" Maeve asked. Still unable to talk, Greg was already enjoying his niece's antics. And he liked the feel of Maeve's arm around his waist. So much, that he returned the favor and slipped his around her too. A smooth move, he thought. Well, sort of, considering that he was crying more than his niece beyond the window.

He saw the picture of course. Everyone was seeing it. "Damn!" he shouted to the walls in his combination living room/bedroom. *How was this happening?* Nervously bouncing from one foot to the other, he'd gone back over everything in his mind. All the details. The only question that mattered at the moment was *Am I safe? Can they find me?* He'd taken all the steps to change his appearance. He was paunchy now, had a flabby gut which he despised. He had some hair since he'd stopped shaving it. Kept it dyed a dark brown. Those were the first things anyone would notice. If they thought he'd been naturally bald, the hair would be the best disguise. But if someone got a close look at him, compared it to the photo which he knew was the employee photo taken not long after he moved to Des Moines, they'd be able to identify him. Even with a different name. He needed to get away. Now. He couldn't delay. He'd stopped pacing, sat at the laptop and went to the travel site he had planned to use, eventually. The new laptop he'd bought after coming back home, having tossed the old one off a bridge so the Iowa cops couldn't use anything in the electronic files against him. He knew there were ways of getting to those files, even if he had deleted them. He booked himself on the soonest flight to take him to Montenegro. It wasn't for two days, he just had to stay undetected for two days. He could do that.

News reports played hourly, the entire city seemed to be on the lookout, but he couldn't be found. A full twenty-hour hours passed. Naturally, the city began to panic. Terrified that there was a killer living there, one who was desperate enough to do anything. Calls to the police report lines flooded in. Too many possible sightings of a thin bald man acting strange. Strange could mean so many things to so many people. Their imaginations ran wild, but at the root of it all was a cold fear for their loved ones. Wives. Daughters. Granddaughters. Girlfriends. She understood that fear. Held it close to her heart too. The only thing more powerful than her fear was her anger.

It was finally here, his Freedom Day. Maybe he'd recognize it every year going forward as a holiday. Do something *special* on the anniversary. The thought made him shake with laughter. He'd planned very well, knew everything was set up on the other end. It would all be ready for him when he arrived. He'd seen the national newscast last night; they had actually dared to speak his name on the report. *Simon Krupp.* Too bad, he'd giggled, that Simon Krupp no longer existed, And, as for the photo they'd shown, the one taken for his employee badge at BICO, well, he looked nothing like that now. There really was nothing that could stop him now. No one would recognize him at the airport. His papers were bullet-proof. He'd giggled again at the pun. *Bullet-proof. I'm really so funny,* he'd thought to himself. He'd paid, and paid a lot of money, to make sure his documentation would stand up to scrutiny. He'd packed the car last night, not that there was much to pack. Most of it he was leaving behind. Let the landlord do with it whatever he wanted. His small carryon was packed only with a few essentials, enough to get him there. If he had stopped to consider, he might have realized that the bag filled only with pairs of socks might strike the airport screener as odd on the x-ray screen. Something like that could make them take a longer look at him. But he hadn't considered. He'd buy whatever else he needed once he arrived, but he had very real concerns about the quality of socks he would be able to buy in Montenegro. The small house he'd rented in advance came furnished, to some degree. What they considered 'furnished' there. A bed and a few chairs around a small table. Not up to his standards, but it was fine. He didn't need more. The house sat about a mile outside of Risan, within view of the sea and with the mountains to its back. It was a good place. Close to the border with Croatia should he need to travel there. He'd studied, had learned that he could buy food locally for next to nothing, really. He might even try growing a few staples himself. He knew that boredom was probably going to be his biggest problem there. Still, it would be entertaining for a while to build his new persona, convince all the locals that he was someone he was not. One expense that he had worked into his plan was for a small boat. It was always good, he thought, to have another means of escape. Small fishing boats were so common there, he'd almost stick out if he *didn't* have one. He might even actually use it to catch some fish to eat. It'd be good practice, learning to control the boat and familiarize himself with the shoreline in both directions, just in case. Turning off the small television set, he glanced, one last time, around the apartment that had served its purpose. Taking his car keys off the nail just inside the front door, he took a deep breath, prepared to completely walk away from his life. It was all going to be so easy.

He turned the lock, walked out onto the small concrete step leading to the sidewalk and his car parked in the road. That was when it hit him. Literally. The first bullet struck him square in the middle of the chest. The second and third and fourth pummeled his body. He was dead before his body even hit the concrete. She wasn't sure if he had even seen her. *Had he known who had ended his life? Who had outsmarted him?* Calmly she sat, placed the 9-1-1 call herself. Confessed, reported what she had done, and waited on the police to arrive. It was over now. Finally, completely over. She had known, of course, all along. Known his secrets. Even as children, she had known his secrets. She'd known what he was doing, even before that day in Des Moines when the police had knocked on her door. She'd pretended ignorance that day, he wasn't the only one who could play a part. It had been so hard, so hard to survive the scandal surrounding Mom's death. Everyone knew that Pops had done it. Simon had been her support then. He'd shielded his sister as much as possible, but it really wasn't possible. When Pops had been killed in prison, she'd suspected. Not that Simon did it, she knew he had not, but that he'd played some role. She'd been angry with him then, seething, because the scandal had all been brought up again. *Why couldn't he just leave things as they were?* Pops would never have gotten out of prison, would have died an old, old man there. She'd been a young mother then, knew that her babies weren't old enough to remember that time, thank goodness. She'd known about his *activities* since then. Had been afraid, constantly, that he would get caught. That even more scandal would erupt. She didn't think she'd survive it again. But he'd been smart. He hadn't gotten caught. She'd believed for a while that everything would be alright. But then he'd started making mistakes. It had all gone downhill when he'd come to Des Moines. The old vagrant that he'd left on the sidewalk, *along with the bat.* That was when she'd first realized he was slipping. She'd watched him closely, seen some of the new habits, knew they were signs of stress. Signs that he was losing some of his grip on reality. The giggling, she wasn't even sure he heard it himself. The cracking of his knuckles, the nervous bouncing from one foot to the other, it was like he couldn't stand still in one place. And then he'd really messed up, messed up bad, with that woman he'd kidnapped, held in his basement. She'd managed to escape. And that had been the real start. The start of the end. It was only a matter of time. They knew his name, had photos of him, knew everything about his background, about *their* family. It was all going to come up again. And this time her sons would be right in the middle of it, trying, as she had done, to just survive it all. The friends who wouldn't be friends anymore. The teachers who would be only too willing to talk about their students. The news reporters constantly peppering them with questions every time they tried to step outside. Having to change schools. Probably having to change names. She was so tired of it, and now it would start again. And not to mention the very fact that both her boys idolized their Uncle. The only man in their life, they'd looked up to him from a very early age. She knew they'd be shattered. She knew where he'd gone, had known he would run back to Providence. It was his favorite hunting ground. The place he had started, the place where he had been on top of his game, the place where he felt safest. She knew about the false name, had made it a point to search his papers and files when he'd taken Jared and James for outings. She knew about the apartment off Federal Hill, the address she'd committed to memory. And she knew that he thought he'd gotten away with everything, would escape now to some backwater country where he could live out his life. And he might. But she'd be left here, trying to put back together the pieces of her life. She'd try, try and fail, she knew, to protect her sons. There was no way to protect them from this. The old scandals would be brought up again, overshadowed only by the scandal of having a brother who was a serial killer. The son of a murderer who had grown up to be a murderer himself. That was just the sort of story the media would love. It would probably end up being made into a movie, or even worse into one of those TV dramas that played constantly on the channels devoted to that sort of thing. It was too late, too late to save herself from what was coming. Too late to save her sons, either. That was why he had to pay. To pay for it all. All the future heartbreak and pain. She would not allow him to escape everything while she and her sons suffered through years of the trauma. The gun had been one of his, one he'd left at her house along with a few other things when he'd disappeared. She'd left the boys with a friend for a few days, a woman she trusted to take care of them. She could only hope that the woman would keep them. There certainly was no other family member for them to go to. But it might be better for them to go to strangers, to get new names, to hopefully survive the system for the next few years, and then to be able to get out and start their lives fresh. Really, it was the only chance for them. It was all she could do for them. To give them the chance, someday, to be normal. *They'd be normal, wouldn't they?*

THE END